YORK NOTES

General Editors: Professor A.N
of Stirling) & Professor Suheil Bushrui (American
University of Beirut)

Scott Fitzgerald

TENDER IS
THE NIGHT

Notes by Gretchen L. Schwenker

BA (WOOSTER, OHIO) PH D (STIRLING)

LONGMAN
YORK PRESS

YORK PRESS
Immeuble Esseily, Place Riad Solh, Beirut.

LONGMAN GROUP UK LIMITED
Longman House, Burnt Mill, Harlow,
Essex CM20 2JE, England
Associated companies, branches and representatives
throughout the world

First published 1984
Third impression 1989

ISBN 0-582-78275-9

Produced by Longman Group (FE) Ltd.
Printed in Hong Kong

Contents

Part 1

Introduction

The life of Scott Fitzgerald

Francis Scott Key Fitzgerald was born in St Paul, Minnesota, in 1896. The Fitzgeralds were a middle-class family, the more affluent side of the family being that of Fitzgerald's mother, who was the daughter of a local merchant, P.F. McQuillan. Much of the attention the young Fitzgerald received in St Paul could be ascribed to this connection, his education being financed with the McQuillan money. His father, Edward Fitzgerald, could trace his Maryland family back to Francis Scott Key (1779–1843), the American lawyer and poet who wrote the words for the national anthem, 'The Star Spangled Banner'. Despite this distinction, Edward Fitzgerald was a middle-class businessman who became more of a failure with each passing year.

Fitzgerald attended a Catholic boarding school, the Newman Academy, at Hackensack, New Jersey, for two years, then in 1915 went to Princeton University in New Jersey, where he became president of the University's Triangle Club, an undergraduate theatrical group which periodically put on an all-male revue. He collaborated in several shows with Edmund Wilson (1895–1972), the writer and critic. At this time Fitzgerald also fell in love with Ginevra King, a young lady from a wealthy Chicago family. This was to prove a bitter experience, and with poor grades in his courses Fitzgerald left for home. He returned to Princeton in 1916, but left the university to join the army in 1917 and so never completed his degree. He served as a lieutenant at a staff headquarters but, to his great disappointment, was never sent overseas. That same year, 1917, he became engaged to another wealthy girl, Zelda Sayre. With Fitzgerald so obviously penniless and as yet unsuccessful in his writing, Zelda became dissatisfied and broke the engagement. In 1919 Fitzgerald began to work as an advertising writer, but left this job to return to St Paul and work on his first novel, *This Side of Paradise*. This was accepted by Scribners, the New York publisher, and published in 1920. Although it received mixed reviews, *This Side of Paradise* became a bestseller; furthermore, it prompted a change of heart in Zelda Sayre, and she and Fitzgerald were married.

Fitzgerald now began selling numerous stories, published his second novel, *The Beautiful and Damned* (1922), and soon found himself the recipient of a considerable income. A daughter Frances was born in

1922 and the family moved into a house on Great Neck, Long Island, taking with them the extravagant way of life which they had rapidly adopted. They went to the French Riviera in 1924, and *The Great Gatsby* was published in 1925. Most of the years between 1924 and 1931 were spent abroad. Fitzgerald had begun to drink and Zelda developed her own problems during these frantic years as she attempted to pursue careers in ballet and writing. She had her first breakdown while abroad in 1930 and the diagnosis was schizophrenia. She suffered a second breakdown in 1932, the year in which her autobiographical novel *Save Me the Waltz* appeared. Despite his drink problem, illness and his wife's difficulties, Fitzgerald began work on *Tender is the Night*, which was eventually published in 1934. That same year Zelda attempted suicide and suffered a final breakdown. She was to remain in clinics for the rest of her life. The following year saw the publication of a further collection of short stories, *Taps at Reveille*, adding to a series of memorable collections published over the previous fifteen years: *Flappers and Philosophers* (1921), *Tales of the Jazz Age* (1922), and *All the Sad Young Men* (1926).

In 1937 Fitzgerald moved to Hollywood and worked as a scriptwriter. Here he fell in love with an actress, Sheilah Graham and in 1939 began work on a new novel, *The Last Tycoon*. But in 1940 he suffered a heart attack and died, leaving the novel uncompleted.

Tender is the Night

Tender is the Night is made up of much that is autobiographical. In many ways the deterioration of its protagonist, Dick Diver, mirrors Fitzgerald's own 'crack-up'. In the collection of essays, letters and notes published posthumously and edited by Edmund Wilson, called *The Crack-up* (1945), Fitzgerald wrote:

> There is another sort of blow that comes from within—that you don't feel until it's too late to do anything about it, until you realise with finality that in some regard you will never be as good a man again. The first sort of breakage seems to happen quick—the second kind happens almost without your knowing it but it is realised suddenly indeed.

The reader is reminded of Dick Diver, broken and beaten in jail in Rome. Dick realises that everything has changed and that he will be a different person because of this experience:

> he had bizarre feelings of what the new self would be. The matter had about it the impersonal quality of an act of God. No mature Aryan is able to profit by a humiliation . . . (Book Two, ch. XXIII)

Dick Diver falls apart under the weight of defeat and humiliation. His drinking leads to a scene in the clinic and to the suggestion that he should leave altogether. There is an unpleasant altercation with his old friend Mary North Minghetti and yet another scene with Lady Caroline Sibly-Biers, then the momentary suggestion of suicide with Nicole and his obvious inability to perform the athletic tricks of his youth on the aquaplane. Rosemary Hoyt informs Dick that she had been told that he had changed and is pleased to see this is untrue, but he replies:

> It is true. . . . The change came a long way back—but at first it didn't show. The manner remains intact for some time after the morale cracks. (Book Three, ch. 7)

When had it begun? The process is suddenly perceived in that humiliation in Rome, but it had started with the pressures of Nicole and the Warren money, and with work left unfinished or neglected on the Riviera amid the beach society. Dick Diver, wanting to be loved, had given too much until there was nothing left. As Fitzgerald wrote in *The Crack-up*:

> The conjuror's hat was empty. To draw things out of it had long been a sort of sleight of hand, and now, to change the metaphor, I was off the dispensing end of the relief roll forever.

In *Tender is the Night*, Fitzgerald portrays a society resembling the society he and his wife knew on the Riviera between 1924 and 1931. His familiarity with bouts of insanity all too obviously reflects his experiences with Zelda. Dick Diver's deterioration is, then, largely Fitzgerald's; both are in pursuit of 'the eternal Carnival by the Sea'.

The strength of the novel, however, lies not only in its poignant autobiographical overtones but in its representation of an era. In this novel the reader re-lives the American Dream, and also watches it fall apart. Fitzgerald has managed to see his personal torment, his bitter experiences, objectively and to place them in the wider context of contemporary society. All points of view are included and add to the effect of the final synthesis. Through the depressing realities that face Dick Diver, the reader can still feel the impact of, for example, the beauty of the Riviera as described in the opening scene. There is greater opportunity for presenting an objective picture when the material being handled does not evoke sympathy; all the more impressive is Fitzgerald's achievement, therefore, in maintaining objectivity with a story as bitter and full of disappointment as this.

Psychoanalysis and the psychological novel

The protagonist of *Tender is the Night* is a psychoanalyst, Dr Richard
Diver. The term psychoanalysis was invented by Sigmund Freud
(1856–1939), the Austrian neurologist. Psychoanalysis came to mean
a method of treating nervous illnesses based on the science of uncon-
scious mental processes. Work in this area was initiated by a Viennese
physician, Josef Breuer (1842–1925), who in 1880–2 discovered a new
way to treat a patient for hysteria through hypnosis. He later worked
with Freud on the subject and their book *Studien über Hysterie*
appeared in 1895. Freud altered the method of treatment by moving
away from hypnosis toward the use of free association. Through what
was referred to as 'catharsis', the patient would be purged, as uncon-
scious mental acts were revealed and replaced by conscious ones.

In 1900 Freud's *Traumdeutung* (The Interpretation of Dreams) was
published. These ideas began to gain acceptance among Swiss psychiatrists in 1907, and in 1908 a meeting in Salzburg brought together those
who agreed with its concepts. Freud and Carl Gustav Jung (1875–
1961) went to the United States in 1909, giving lectures on psychoanalysis at Clark University. Freud wrote other works on psychoanalysis,
including *Three Contributions to the Theory of Sex* (1905), *Beyond the
Pleasure Principle* (1920) and *The Collected Papers of Sigmund Freud*
(1924).

This new science had a considerable influence on the literature of the
time. With its emphasis on sexual study, psychoanalysis allowed for
greater discussion of sexual relationships, and its impact on the treatment of this topic in literature became clearly recognisable after the
First World War. Numerous psychoanalytical studies of the lives of
writers and artists appeared at this time, including Freud's own *Leo-
nardo da Vinci: A Psychosexual Study of an Infantile Reminiscence*
(1910) and René Laforgue's *The Defeat of Baudelaire: A Psycho-
Analytical Study of the Neurosis of Charles Baudelaire* (1931). Psychoanalysis had a great effect on criticism, and was introduced into the
novel. Thomas Mann, for example, made use of the new science in his
novel *The Magic Mountain* (1924). Thus we find an analyst as the
central character in Fitzgerald's *Tender is the Night*, and Nicole, the
analyst's troubled wife, becomes the perfect character through which
to explore the principles of psychoanalysis.

A note on the text

Tender is the Night was first published by Scribners, New York, in
1934. The book was neither popularly nor critically a great success.
Fitzgerald reacted to this by beginning to revise the novel toward the
end of 1938. The major change which he wanted to make was to move

the middle part of the book, where we meet young Dr Diver in Switzerland, to the beginning. There are other minor revisions and corrections
which Fitzgerald wrote into his personal copy of the 1934 edition. This
revised version was posthumously published by Scribners in 1953 as the
second of *Three Novels*. However, Fitzgerald's personal copy of the
novel in which he made those corrections also shows clearly that he
intended to revise the novel further. As Malcolm Cowley pointed out in
his introduction to the revised version, Fitzgerald had written in at the
end of chapter 2, 'This is my mark to say that I have made final corrections up to this point.' It is difficult to say what further changes Fitzgerald would have made, and so, rather than deal with this unfinished
version, the original of 1934 is the version discussed in these Notes. The
text used is *Tender is the Night*, volume II of 'The Bodley Head Scott
Fitzgerald', The Bodley Head, London, 1961, and references are to
this edition.

Part 2

Summaries
of TENDER IS THE NIGHT

A general summary

The story opens on the French Riviera, where Gausse's Hotel has become a fashionable summer resort. In the summer of 1925 Rosemary Hoyt, a seventeen-year-old film actress, and her mother, Mrs Elsie Speers, arrive for a holiday. Rosemary meets several people on the beach: one group comprises Señor Campion, Mrs Abrams, Mr and Mrs Albert McKisco, and Mr Dumphry; and making up another are Dick Diver and his wife Nicole, Abe and Mary North, and Tommy Barban. Rosemary is particularly attracted to Dick Diver who seems to be the focal point of the latter group. She is convinced that she has fallen in love with him.

Dick Diver gives a party at the Villa Diana, the Divers' home. During the evening, Mrs McKisco discovers something upstairs in the bathroom which is revealing about Nicole. Tommy Barban tells her to keep quiet. Rosemary is invited by Dick to accompany their group to Paris to see Abe North off to America. The guests drive home in two cars and Rosemary learns from Campion that there is going to be a duel between Tommy Barban and McKisco. Abe North explains that the fight began over Mrs McKisco's attempt to tell everyone in their car what she had seen in the bathroom. Rosemary and Campion attend the duel in which neither man is harmed.

In Paris Dick tries to bring the various members of the group together as a social unit. Rosemary witnesses a scene that makes her realise that Dick and Nicole still have a strong attraction for each other. Rosemary tells Dick she loves him, but when she asks him to make love to her, he resists. However, the following day Dick tells Rosemary that he loves her too, but their relationship remains unaltered on account of his continuing love for Nicole.

Abe North, who has become an alcoholic, prepares to leave for America. At the station, shots are fired at an Englishman by Maria Wallis, a girl the Divers know. They are shocked. The romance between Dick and Rosemary continues, and Dick Diver is greatly disturbed by revelations about her lack of innocence provided by Rosemary's friend, Collis Clay. The following morning Nicole awakes to a knock at her hotel bedroom door and finds the police looking for Abe North. Abe has returned to Paris and is involved in an altercation with three negroes. One of these men arrives with Abe at the Divers' hotel. Abe and his companion find Dick in Rosemary's room and try to explain Abe's quarrel and the difficulties it has created for the Negro, Jules Peterson. After Abe has left, Rosemary discovers Peterson dead in her room. Dick moves the body into the corridor to protect Rosemary's career, but suddenly Nicole, who is involved in this transfer, breaks down and becomes insanely hysterical in the bathroom. Rosemary now understands what it was that Mrs McKisco saw.

Th story then moves back in time, to Zurich in 1917. A young psychologist named Richard Diver arrives there to study. In 1914 he had gone to Oxford as a Rhodes scholar. The next year he returned home and took his degree at Johns Hopkins University. He went to Vienna in 1916 to do further study and to write some pamphlets. After completing his next degree with more research in Zurich in 1917, he joined a neurological unit at Bar-sur-Aube, France. Discharged in the Spring of 1919 he returns to Zurich to visit Franz Gregorovious at Professor Dohmler's clinic, which had been considered the first modern clinic for mental illness when it had been founded ten years before. There he becomes involved in helping a patient, Nicole Warren, to recover from schizophrenia. She is the wealthy daughter of Devereux Warren, whose incestuous act with his daughter had brought about her illness. Nicole falls in love with Dick Diver, and he is advised to end the relationship. He does so but meets Nicole again while on holiday in Caux. Baby Warren, her sister, tells him that the Warre family would like nothing better than if she could fall in love with a doctor who could take care of her. To Dick, this sounds as if the Warrens are going to 'buy' Nicole a doctor with their great wealth and influence. Despite the revulsion he feels at this thought, Dick finds himself in love with Nicole. Against the wishes of Baby Warren, who in fact finds Dick socially inferior, they marry. Nicole experiences two major recurrences of her illness during the first years of their marriage. They have two children, Lanier and Topsy, and go to live on the Riviera.

The story now returns to the present, continuing the former narrative. At the Villa Diana in August, Dick braces himself to see Nicole. They had left Paris shortly after her new attack. Dick tries not to let Nicole know how he feels about Rosemary. He also feels increasingly restricted by the Warren money which supports them. In December, they go on a winter holiday in the Swiss Alps and are joined by Baby Warren. Dick meets Franz Gregorovious there, and despite Dick's resentment at using Warren money to finance the project, agrees to join Franz as a partner in a clinic on the Zugersee in Switzerland. At the clinic, Dick is popular with patients and Nicole helps in designing the buildings. However, during a family outing Nicole makes a scene over a letter which accuses Dick of seducing the daughter of a patient. She loses control and causes an accident by grabbing the wheel of the car. Overwhelmed by this last incident, Dick leaves the clinic for a while. He meets Tommy Barban in Munich and learns that Abe North has been beaten to death in a speak-easy (an illicit bar) in New York. A cable arrives with news of the death of Dick's father, and he goes home for the funeral. On his way back he meets Albert McKisco, now a successful novelist, on the ship. The McKiscos leave the ship at Gibraltar and Dick goes to Rome, where he meets Rosemary and Collis Clay, and on this occasion he finally makes love to Rosemary. He also meets Baby Warren in Rome. Dick realises he is not in love with Rosemary; furthermore he finds that she is having an affair with the leading man in her latest film. Dick retreats from the affair, and, Rosemary having arranged to leave Rome the next day, he goes drinking with Collis Clay. Later, when Dick tries to get back to his hotel, he becomes involved in an argument with some taxi-drivers. He is taken to a police station to settle the matter, loses his temper and unwittingly hits a plainclothes policeman. As a result he is badly beaten up and thrown into jail. Dick is finally rescued through the efforts of Baby Warren, who is pleased to gain a sense of moral superiority over him.

At the clinic, Franz's wife, Kaethe, works to get rid of the Divers and finally convinces Franz that Dick is no longer a 'serious' doctor and has begun to drink heavily. Dick is sent away on a case to help a Señor Pardo y Ciudad Real with his alcoholic, homosexual son. He meets Royal Dumphry who informs him that Devereux Warren is dying in Lausanne. Warren wants to see his daughter and Dick promises to consult Franz as to whether this should be arranged. Nicole learns from Kaethe that her father is dying and goes to Lausanne, only to find that he has recovered enough to have left the city. At the clinic, the father of a patient angrily removes his son from their care and accuses Dick of drinking excessively. Dick is shaken and resolves to change; but when Franz hears of the incident, Dick suddenly finds himself agreeing to leave the clinic.

Before returning to the Riviera, the Divers visit Mary North, now Mary Minghetti, who has married a wealthy Asian with a papal title. The visit ends abruptly with a quarrel between Dick and Mary over a misunderstanding about Lanier, the Divers' son. Upon returning to the Villa Diana, the relationship between Dick and Nicole breaks down still further and she suggests that she has ruined him. At a party on a yacht Nicole meets Tommy Barban. Dick has a scene with Lady Caroline Sibly-Biers and also acts as if he is going to commit suicide with Nicole by jumping overboard. Tommy drives them home from Cannes and the next morning the two men both feel concerned about Nicole. Nicole realises that she dislikes Dick and that Tommy loves her. To Dick's displeasure, she gives Tommy a special jar of camphor rub as he leaves.

accent above, see ms

In June, Nicole learns that Tommy is in Nice; Rosemary also returns to the Riviera. The Divers meet Rosemary on the beach and Dick attempts to impress her by trying aquaplane stunts which he has become too old to execute successfully. Nicole is disgusted. They meet Mary North on the beach; Nicole exchanges bitter comments with Rosemary and leaves to write a note to Tommy. The next day Nicole finds a note from Dick telling her that he will be away for a few days. Tommy calls to say he is coming over to visit her. Nicole and Tommy go to a small hotel by the sea and make love. They are interrupted by a group of noisy American sailors leaving their girlfriends or prostitutes, and so they leave the hotel and take a late-night swim before Nicole returns to the Villa Diana. Dick arrives home the next day and tells her that he now realises that Rosemary is still immature. Tommy calls and insists that Dick must learn the truth. Nicole and Dick argue, and the scene ends with Nicole and Dick free of each other at last. Late that night, Dick rescues Mary North and Lady Caroline Sibly-Biers from the police.

Tommy Barban confronts Dick at the barber's the next day, and with Nicole they go to the Café des Alliés. It is decided that Dick and Nicole will divorce. To Tommy's surprise there is no fight. Nicole realises that Dick has known the truth since the camphor rub episode. Dick spends time with the children before he leaves. On the beach he has some drinks with Mary North whom he momentarily considers seducing. Nicole wants to go to help him when she sees him having difficulty getting up after so much drinking, but she is restrained by Tommy.

Nicole marries Tommy; she keeps in touch with Dick who opens a series of offices in small towns in the United States with mixed success. Their lives follow their separate courses, and as time goes by they hear less and less of each other.

Detailed summaries
BOOK ONE

Chapter I

On the French Riviera, five miles from Cannes, there is a hotel, Gausse's Hôtel des Étrangers, which has become a fashionable summer resort. In June 1925 a girl who is almost eighteen years old arrives there with her mother. She is Rosemary Hoyt, a young film actress. On the beach Rosemary meets several people, including Señor Campion, Mrs Abrams, Mr and Mrs McKisco and Mr Royal Dumphry. They recognise who she is and warn her about getting sunburnt.

NOTES AND GLOSSARY:

victoria: an open car or carriage with a collapsible cover over the passenger seat

flotte: (*French*) fleet

Chapter II

Rosemary is told obliquely by Mrs McKisco that they thought she was 'in the plot', a reference to some kind of game which the group is playing. Rosemary finds she dislikes these people and she watches a group on the other side of the beach. Mrs McKisco mentions that one of the group is Abe North, 'a rotten musician'; another is Mrs Diver. She is highly critical of their circle, but Rosemary notices with interest the man wearing a jockey cap. This is Dick Diver. Rosemary falls asleep in the sun and when she wakes finds the beach deserted but for Diver, who shows his concern that she will become painfully sunburnt.

NOTES AND GLOSSARY:

tow-headed: flaxen-haired; with fair, tousled hair

Antheil and Joyce: George Antheil (1900–59) was an American composer and pianist. His dissonant, boisterous compositions such as the 'Airplane Sonata' caused much controversy. However, major writers of the day such as Joyce, Yeats and Pound championed him. James Joyce (1882–1941) was an Irish novelist best-known for his controversial work, *Ulysses*, first published in Paris in 1922 and now considered a masterpiece of modern fiction

He's got insides: Mrs McKisco is using an American colloquial expression meaning that a person has depth of character, not just a superficial façade. The expression implies feelings and a thoughtful nature. She addresses this remark to her husband who is a writer and critic

peignoir: (*French*) dressing or bathing gown

the man in the jockey cap: this is Rosemary's second look at Dick Diver. From the start she is attracted by his charm and his own kind of celebrity. She first observes him 'giving a . . . little performance' in chapter I

Chapter III

Over lunch at the hotel Rosemary tells her mother that she has fallen in love with Dick Diver on the beach, but mentions that he is married. Her mother, Mrs Elsie Speers, is also her best friend. Mrs Speers believes that Rosemary must now learn to stand on her own. She reminds her that she should go to Monte Carlo to see Earl Brady, a film director. Later Rosemary leaves for Cannes where by chance she again sees Mrs Diver. The next day Rosemary and her mother go for a drive along the coast. In the evening Rosemary thinks again about the people on the beach and decides to spend no more time with the first group she had met.

NOTES AND GLOSSARY:

talking loud Italian: Cannes is near the Italian border

table d'hôte: (*French*) literally, 'host's table'; a meal served to guests at a fixed time and price

Daddy's Girl: Rosemary's first film, making her a young starlet

sudden flatness...quiet foreign places: taken out of what is considered a culture with a fast pace, Americans can find themselves rather lost. In the frenetic boom of the twenties, this change must have been all the more apparent

Gausse *père*: the owner of the hotel. He appears near the end of the book (see Book Three, ch. X)

métier: (*French*) profession or trade

Pont du Gard: a three-tiered Roman aqueduct

hacks: cabs, taxis

chow: a Chinese breed of dog which has a full ruff of long hair

Café des Alliés: this is the setting used later for the final confrontation between Dick Diver, Tommy Barban and Nicole near the end of Book Three. It is also the location of Dick's talk with Mrs Speers about Rosemary in Book Two, ch. XI

cosmopolites: people with wide, international sophistication and attitudes, free from provincial limitations

Le Temps: one of the foremost French daily newspapers of the time

The Saturday Evening Post: an American magazine; it published many of Fitzgerald's short stories during the twenties and thirties

The chauffeur...Ivan the Terrible: a fanciful reference to the fate of the Russian aristocracy after the Bolshevik revolution of 1917. Many of those who escaped from Russia left without much wealth and took menial positions in their adopted countries in order to survive. Ivan the Terrible was Ivan IV Vasilievich (1530–84), ruler of Russia (1533–84) and crowned the first Czar in 1547

Ten years ago:	the reader can assume this refers precisely to 1917; thus the story must be taking place in 1927
agates and cornelian:	precious stones. Agates typically have colours arranged in stripes. Cornelian, or carnelian, has a reddish colour
green milk:	milk that has not been pasteurised
estaminets:	small cafés or bistros
Corniche d'Or:	the road built along the coast. From Nice to Menton, one can take the corniche along the sea
plage:	(*French*) beach

Chapter IV

On the beach the next morning Rosemary finds that the McKiscos are not there, and Dick Diver invites her over to his group. She meets his wife Nicole and learns from Abe North and Nicole that it was the Divers who had really laid the foundations for the popularity of the resort by building a house nearby. Rosemary also notices the younger, bored Tommy Barban. She realises that these are fashionable people. She considers the three men and admires Dick Diver most, and Nicole notices this admiration. The McKiscos and their group arrive on the beach and are criticised by Rosemary's new friends. However, against Nicole's wishes, Dick Diver decides to invite the other group to dinner. They swim and then Dick tries on a pair of black lace drawers which Nicole has been making. This creates a stir among the McKisco group. Rosemary enjoys the carefree behaviour of her companions and admires the way of life which the Divers lead; she is not yet aware of the difficulties they must overcome to present this face to the world. Later, with her mother, Rosemary cries over her love for Dick, but responds immediately when reminded that love should bring happiness. Rosemary tells her mother that they have been invited to dinner by the Divers at the end of the week.

NOTES AND GLOSSARY:

He broke down:	an American colloquial expression, meaning that Dick ceased to be impersonal and allowed himself to express his interest and concern, giving way to his real instincts
Rodinesque:	in the style of the French sculptor, François Auguste René Rodin (1840–1917)
garçon:	(*French*) waiter
chasseur:	(*French*) literally, 'hunter' or 'huntsman'; here, a liveried attendant or footman
The young man of Latin aspect:	Tommy Barban

New York Herald: an American newspaper of excellent quality which finally ceased publication in the 1960s

Mrs Evelyn Oyster ... Mr S. Flesh: these names are meant to be absurd and amusing in a parody of the society of the time and the constant stream of Americans arriving in Europe to spend their excess of money. Fitzgerald delights in this kind of exaggeration

drones: male honey bees which do not work; hence, people who live on the labours of others, parasites

the Yale prom: the formal autumn dance at Yale University, New Haven, Connecticut. Yale is also referred to in the book simply as 'New Haven'

gourmandise: (*French*) a fondness for good food and drink

pansy: a slang expression for a homosexual

a desperate bargain with the gods: this is the first real indication Fitzgerald gives us that all is not well with the Divers and that Rosemary's romantic impressions may be totally incorrect

---

Chapter V

Rosemary goes to Monte Carlo to meet Earl Brady and is taken to his film set. Brady compliments her on her role in *Daddy's Girl*, and wants to make a film with her. They are attracted to each other. Mrs Speers is pleased with Rosemary's account of the day's events but still considers that Rosemary needs to be more independent.

NOTES AND GLOSSARY:

an old Gaumont lot: Leon Gaumont (1864–1946), a French pioneer film executive and inventor, established the Gaumont Company in 1895. Later, his company expanded to include studios and cinemas in Paris and elsewhere

autochthonous: indigenous, native

amaranth, mimosa: amaranth includes any of a large genus of coarse herbs with showy flowers, such as Prince's Feather. Mimosa is a kind of shrub with round heads of small white or yellow flowers

flats: stage scenery

fifteen pounds ... cockney accent: Earl Brady is obviously English. Cockney is a London accent, particularly of the east end

First National ... Famous: Hollywood film studios

espadrilles: light summer shoes

Chapter VI

Nicole Diver goes for a walk in her garden. Dick tells her that he has invited Mrs Abrams and wants to give 'a really *bad* party'. Dick is in a mood which first creates an excitement that buoys up those around him but later leaves him slightly depressed. To be included in Dick's world is a special and memorable experience.

That evening Dick greets his guests, among whom is Earl Brady. The Divers' children, Lanier and Topsy, sing for the guests. Rosemary feels that the Divers' house, the Villa Diana, is like a stage where something significant could occur. She has a conversation with Tommy Barban, who tells her that he leaves to fight a war in the morning, and that a short stay with the Divers always makes him want to go to war. He is clearly a mercenary. Rosemary knows that her mother approves of her feelings for Dick Diver, and she declares her love for him. His reply is ambiguous.

NOTES AND GLOSSARY:

cabinet de toilette : (*French*) dressing room

leaving . . . said or done: compare this with the end of the book. Dick Diver seems to fade away, becoming totally inessential

Au clair de la lune . . . : (*French*) 'In the moonlight/ My friend Pierrot/ Lend me your pen/ To write a note/ My candle is burnt out/ I have no more light/ Open the door for me/ For the love of God'

the profanity of his bitterness: Rosemary's simple, happy picture of the Divers and their society is once again disproved. Tommy Barban's relationship with them is far more complex than she had realised and we are made aware of his feelings for Nicole. The duel naturally follows

Chapter VII

Nicole sits between Tommy Barban and Abe North, and Rosemary listens to their bizarre conversation. Everyone, with the exception of McKisco, an author and critic, falls under the Divers' spell. Rosemary enjoys the whole scene and the sense of affection imparted by the Divers. She feels that she belongs here, that this is her spiritual home.

Nicole, rather enigmatically, gives Rosemary's mother a yellow handbag and various yellow articles before disappearing into the house. The guests go on to the terrace and Violet McKisco leaves them to go to the bathroom. Rosemary listens to an argument between

Barban and McKisco, a clash of their different worlds: Barban the mercenary, McKisco the unsuccessful writer. Mrs McKisco returns excitedly to say that she has witnessed an amazing scene upstairs but Tommy Barban interrupts her and prevents her from revealing more.

NOTES AND GLOSSARY:

cater-cornered: in a diagonal or oblique position, diagonally across

Veuve Cliquot: a champagne

arriviste: (*French*) Violet McKisco's husband Al is a writer and critic but without much repute. *Arriviste* means one that is a new and uncertain arrival, as in society or art

Mrs Burnett's vicious tracts: Frances Hodgson Burnett (1849–1924) was an American novelist, born in England. She wrote such favourite romantic tales as *That Lass o' Lowrie's* (1877), *Through One Administration* (1883) and (her most famous), *Little Lord Fauntleroy* (1886). Fitzgerald's sarcasm may stem from the last of these

the Riff: Berbers of the Riff in northern Morocco. France and Spain both had protectorates in Morocco. Abdel Krim, a Riffian leader, led a successful revolt against the Spanish in 1921, and in 1925 invaded the French protectorate. A joint Franco-Spanish force defeated him in 1926 and he surrendered to France

the 'Harvard manner': as in Harvard University, Cambridge, Massachusetts. The Harvard undergraduates affected the manners of the British upper-class

Chapter VIII

Dick returns and separates Barban and the McKiscos, re-establishing the calm of the evening. He and Rosemary look out over the Mediterranean, and Dick asks Rosemary if she would like to go to Paris with them to see Abe and Mary North off to America. When she learns that her mother has consented to the idea, Rosemary agrees enthusiastically. She tells him again that she had fallen in love with him the first time she saw him, and in his guarded response he tells her that she does not know what she wants. As she leaves with her mother and the other guests, Rosemary wonders what Mrs McKisco saw in the bathroom.

NOTES AND GLOSSARY:

a Fourth-of-July balloon: a reference to the celebration of Independence Day in the United States

chasuble: the sleeveless outer vestment worn at mass by a priest

Isotta: an Italian car, the Milanese Isotta-Fraschini car. This small company sold most of its luxury cars to Americans in the years just before and after the First World War

Chapter IX

The two cars, one Brady's and the other the Divers', follow each other back to the hotel, but the Divers' car slows down and Brady's passes it. At the hotel Rosemary lies awake, disturbed by her new freedom from her mother. We hear of Mrs Speers's firm, if unorthodox, attitude to her daughter and her career. Rosemary finds Luis Campion weeping on the stairway, saying that people who love suffer. He tells her that Abe North is at the hotel, then reveals, with some relish, that a duel between Barban and McKisco has been arranged for five o'clock that morning. Abe North appears and Campion leaves. Rosemary asks Abe about the duel.

NOTES AND GLOSSARY:

Will you kaindlay stup tucking! : meant to suggest a clipped, aristocratic English voice

sewing-circle member: a sarcastic use of the term, deriding Campion's effeminacy. Ladies in small American towns would often form sewing circles where they would sew together and enjoy gossip

Chapter X

Abe informs Rosemary that when Earl Brady's car passed the Divers', Violet McKisco was hinting to Mrs Abrams about what she had discovered about the Divers, and Tommy had asked her to refrain. The car had stopped and Barban had begun yelling at McKisco, who in turn had suggested that there should be a 'code duello'. Then Tommy had struck him. Back at the hotel the two parties had remained firm in their resolve. Rosemary asks if the Divers know the cause of the duel and is told that they do not. Rosemary and Abe go to see McKisco who gives Abe an envelope marked 'For my wife'; he makes a pathetic picture of failure, but none the less feels he cannot back out of the duel. Abe gives him Barban's duelling pistols; a combination of their antiquity and the agreed distance at which they are to be fired will ensure that the duel will not be fatal. Before leaving, Rosemary again appeals to them to call it off. McKisco asks to see Abe alone.

NOTES AND GLOSSARY:
bromide: a sedative

Chapter XI

Rosemary finds Campion downstairs in the hotel; he asks her to go to watch the duel with him. Rosemary refuses, but her mother suggests that she should go and so she accepts Campion's offer. They drive to the golf course and watch at a distance. McKisco drinks brandy from a bottle. In the duel neither shot finds its target. Barban still wants satisfaction, but Abe North, who is acting as McKisco's second, steps in on McKisco's behalf and refuses a second round. As they leave McKisco congratulates himself on his courage. Abe is considerably less impressed by the whole affair. McKisco is then sick, Campion lies on his back gasping with trepidation and Rosemary is overcome with laughter. She looks forward to seeing Dick again.

NOTES AND GLOSSARY:
Pardon, Messieurs...: (*French*) 'Excuse me, gentlemen... Would you mind paying my fees? It's only for medical attention of course. Mr Barban has only got a thousand [franc] note and can't pay the fees, and the other one has left his wallet at home.'

Chapter XII

Rosemary, Dick, the Norths and two French musicians are waiting for Nicole at a restaurant called Voisins in Paris. Dick claims playfully that he is the only American with 'repose'. Rosemary is sure he is right, and is happy to feel a part of a group which is drawn together by Dick. She enjoys the lunch party but afterwards is startled to overhear a private conversation between Dick and Nicole that demonstrates their passionate feelings for each other and in which they arrange to meet at their hotel later that afternoon to make love. Rosemary and Nicole go shopping together and Nicole, in buying quite casually an extensive array of luxuries and gifts, is seen as fulfilling her role in the vast system of production that supports her. When Nicole remembers her arrangement to meet Dick, Rosemary feels resentful.

NOTES AND GLOSSARY:
at Voisins: they are now in Paris
West Point: the United States Military Academy at West Point, New York. Abe is hoping that this tough military training will have created his 'man with repose'

coup de grâce: (*French*) a decisive finishing blow, act, or event

vestiaire: (*French*) cloakroom

the product of much ingenuity and toil: Fitzgerald has gone to great lengths in this description of Nicole's buying to underline the harshness of the capitalist system of which she is a product. He also wants to show how well she fits in this role and the casual grace with which she wears it

chicle factories: chewing gum factories. Chicle is a gum from the latex of the sapodilla which is the main ingredient in chewing gum

the Five-and-Tens: shops in America that originally sold merchandise costing no more than five or ten cents. A shop such as Woolworths still selling mainly inexpensive items might be referred to as a 'Five-and-Ten' or 'Five and Dime'

Chapter XIII

Dick, Nicole, Rosemary and Abe North visit the First World War trenches near Beaumont Hamel and the hill of Thiepval. Dick talks of the vast casualties of the war and Rosemary, now desperately in love, listens attentively. Abe North is less inclined to be moved, and counters Dick's seriousness by placing the First World War in the wider context of death and history; but when he jokes Dick refuses to respond. Rosemary, under the spell of Dick's sombre mood, cries at a memorial. On their journey back, Dick sees a girl from Tennessee whom they had met that morning, holding a wreath brought for her dead brother. She cannot find his grave, and so Dick suggests that she lay it on any grave near by. Rosemary cries again. They return to Amiens and take the train to Paris.

NOTES AND GLOSSARY:

Thiepval: a German stronghold northeast of Amiens, captured by the British in August 1918 near the end of the First World War

Turkey ... Morocco: Mustafa Kemal led Turkish nationalists in resisting Italian, French and Greek military advances from 1919 to 1923. For the action in Morocco, see the note on 'Riff', p.19

Marne: a river in northeast France which flows west into the Seine. In the first battle of the Marne, September 1914, the British and French halted the German advance on Paris. Each side suffered half a million casualties

Crown Prince:	Friedrich Wilhelm Victor August Ernst, Crown Prince of Germany (1889–1918)

Unter den Linden: the main boulevard of Berlin

mairie: (*French*) town hall

Petersburg: Petersburg was besieged by the Unionist forces in the final stages of the American Civil War. The loss of lives was enormous on both sides and the siege in many ways foreshadowed the trench warfare of the First World War

Lewis Carroll: Charles Lutwidge Dodgson (1832–98), English mathematician and writer, author of *Alice's Adventures in Wonderland*

Jules Verne: (1828–1905) French author of adventure stories which helped to popularise science, including *Voyage au centre de la terre* (1864) and *Vingt mille lieues sous les mers* (1870)

Undine: possibly referring to *Ondine* by Jean Giraudoux (1882–1944), French novelist and dramatist

marraines: (*French*) literally, godmother or presenter (as of a debutante), a sponsor. In war, *marraine de guerre* refers to a correspondent of a soldier

the last love battle: Fitzgerald is mixing the theme of love 'mingled with savagery and war'. Later, Dick's own 'lovely safe world' would blow up with love of an explosive kind. Tommy Barban's relationship with Nicole certainly mixes the two

the silver cord ... broken: 'Or ever the silver cord be loosed, or the golden bowl be broken, or the pitcher be broken at the fountain, or the wheel broken at the cistern. Then shall the dust return to the earth as it was: and the spirit shall return unto God who gave it' (see the Bible, Ecclesiastes 12:5–7)

men arguing with a hundred *voilàs*: this shows the intensity and excitement Fitzgerald sees in this French culture. *Voilà* is an exclamation; literally 'look there'

Württembergers, ... old Etonians: a reference to different groups of war graves. The gloom in this chapter seems to forbode Dick's personal disaster

---

Chapter XIV

In Paris, Nicole is tired and stays at the hotel; this makes Rosemary feel better, although she begins to acknowledge the force of Nicole's personality. She goes with Dick and the Norths to a houseboat café on the Seine. Abe is drinking and his wife chides him. He gives champagne to Rosemary, who announces that the previous day was her eighteenth birthday. Mary speaks of future plans: Abe will go to America, Mary to Munich. Dick then announces that he may abandon the scientific treatise he is writing.

Chapter XV

Rosemary goes home with Dick. Only now does she discover that his profession is medicine. Again she tells him she loves him. Dick, somewhat taken aback by her advances, kisses her reluctantly and thinks of her youth and innocence. He feels that she is not ready for the affair she is inviting. At the hotel, Rosemary asks him directly to make love to her, but Dick senses she is playing a role and blames the champagne. Rosemary persists, but Dick refuses and leaves in some confusion.

Chapter XVI

Rosemary wakes up ashamed, not looking forward to meeting the Divers. She shops with Nicole and feels jealous. When Rosemary sees Dick at lunch, she knows all is well, and that Dick is beginning to fall in love with her. They go to Franco-American Films to see a showing of Rosemary in *Daddy's Girl*, and a friend of Rosemary's, Collis Clay, joins them. Dick says Rosemary will become one of the best actresses, and she announces that she has arranged a screen test for him. Dick turns this down firmly, but later he is flattered by her hopes that he might one day have been her leading man in a film. Then they are alone again; Dick is taking her to a tea party which he feels Rosemary will not enjoy.

NOTES AND GLOSSARY:

our Lake Forest House: Lake Forest is on Lake Michigan, north of Chicago

apache: in Paris, a member of a group of criminals, a hooligan

I have not any benenas: an unsuccessful attempt to copy American slang taken from the popular song, 'Yes, We have No Bananas'

Duncan Phyfe: an American cabinet maker (1768–1854), born in Scotland, who opened a shop in New York City in 1790. His furniture showed his adaptations of Sheraton and Adam, helping to create the furniture of the American Federal period. Interest in Duncan Phyfe furniture revived in the 1920s and 1930s

Chapter XVII

The house they go to is so stylish and modern that it gives Rosemary the sense of being on a film set. Dick and Rosemary are separated and Rosemary hears a trio of women discussing the Divers and their crowd. She is indignant and looks for Dick. They leave, and in doing so Dick indicates that he feels badly about their own personal situation. Rosemary breaks into sobs. They both say they love each other, but Dick feels there is nothing to be done because he also loves Nicole and because of the complications an affair would involve. He mentions the duel and explains that Nicole is not very strong.

NOTES AND GLOSSARY:

Cardinal de Retz: a French ecclesiastic and politician (1614–79)

Decorative Arts Exhibition: the house and the people in it are meant to be characteristic of the 'art-deco' era—'modern', empty and false. Rosemary has the feeling of being on a film set

Louisa M. Alcott: an American author (1832–88), whose best-known novel is *Little Women* (1868)

Madame de Ségur: Sophie Rostopchine, Comtesse de Ségur (1799–1874), born in Russia, was a writer of children's books. An edition of her works was published in 1930–2

Chapter XVIII

Dick's party is in high spirits that evening and they drive all over Paris, part of the time in a luxurious car belonging to the Shah of Persia. Rosemary is very happy; she dances with Dick and they play a joke at the Ritz by pretending that Abe North is General Pershing, and then build a 'waiter trap' out of furniture. Rosemary promises to help Mary North to get Abe home and so does not leave with Dick and Nicole when they offer to take her back to the hotel. Rosemary then leaves with the others and rides in a market wagon full of carrots; for a time dejected, she suddenly feels elated when she sees a horse-chestnut tree in bloom being transported to the Champs-Élysées.

NOTES AND GLOSSARY:

the car of the Shah of Persia: Reza Khan ruled Persia (Iran) after his 1921 coup and was Shah from 1925. He centralised control and created the façade of a modern state

Major Hengest and Mr Horsa: Abe is frivolously alluding to the brothers Hengist and Horsa, the reputed leaders of the Jute invaders of Britain about 449 AD

Pershing:	an American general (1860–1948) who commanded the U.S. expeditionary forces in the First World War
Goldberg:	Rube Goldberg (1883–1970), a cartoonist

Chapter XIX

The following morning, Abe, very much the worse for wear, is about to leave from the Gare Saint-Lazare. Nicole arrives to see him off, but Abe speaks unpleasantly to her. Nicole is unsympathetic to his self-pitying and aggressive mood and criticises him for his drinking. With some relief she sees a girl whom she knows and rushes away to speak to her, but soon returns, disgruntled by the girl's cold reaction. Rosemary and Mary North appear, and all the women are pleased when Dick arrives to dispel the oppression caused by Abe North's presence. As Abe's train draws away, shots are fired by the girl to whom Nicole had just spoken. Dick discovers that Maria Wallis, as the girl is called, has shot an Englishman, and he decides that he ought to go to see her at the police station; but Nicole recommends that the best thing would be to telephone the girl's sister. Left alone as Nicole makes the phone call, Rosemary and Dick are reminded of their love for each other. All are shocked by the violence of the shooting, but leave the station almost as if nothing had occurred.

NOTES AND GLOSSARY:

the Crystal Palace:	made of iron and glass and designed by Sir Joseph Paxton, the Crystal Palace was first erected in Hyde Park in 1851, then moved to south London in 1854. There it served as an amusement centre for the next quarter of a century
Diaghilev:	Sergei Pavlovich Diaghilev (1872–1929), Russian art critic and celebrated ballet producer. Dick's remarks are, of course, sarcastic
Tu as vu . . . :	(*French*) 'Did you notice the revolver? It was very small, a real pearl, a toy.' 'But powerful enough! . . . Did you see his shirt? Enough blood to make you think you were in a war.'

Chapter XX

They have lunch; both Rosemary and Dick feel unhappy. Mary North leaves to take her train to Salzburg and Rosemary also departs. Dick sees some unhappiness in Nicole's expression and wonders what she thinks. Collis Clay arrives at the restaurant and Nicole leaves. Collis tells Dick a story about Rosemary and a friend of his being caught in a

locked railway compartment by the conductor (guard), in the act of
some imprecise misdemeanour. The implications stun Dick, for they
reveal that Rosemary may not be so innocent as he has been given to
believe. Dick goes to his bank, cashing his cheque with the man he feels
will least notice his troubled demeanour, and suddenly leaves in a taxi
for the Films Par Excellence studio. He is confused by recent events,
aware that what he is now doing marks a turning-point in his life, and
compelled irresistibly forward by subconscious forces beyond his
control.

NOTES AND GLOSSARY:

people he had 'worked over': this shows Dick's constant need to be
involved with people and to nurture them. It is a
need to be loved that finally leaves him empty and
defeated

Grand Guignol: 'Guignol' refers to a marionette first introduced
into outdoor puppet shows about 1815 by Laurent
Mourquet (1745–1844). Children's puppet
theatres in Paris are called *théâtres de Guignol*.
From these innocent beginnings there somehow
came about the *Théâtre de Grand Guignol* which
specialised in plays of horror and violence

fraternity politics: a student organisation or club for men at an
American university is referred to as a 'fraternity'.
Named with Greek letters, these groups are active
socially and have secret rites

Brentano's: a New York bookshop

Tarkington: Booth Tarkington (1869–1946), an American
novelist whose works include *Seventeen*, *Alice
Adams* and *Penrod*

Papeterie . . . : (*French*) 'Stationery', 'Bakery', 'Clearance Sale',
'Special Offer', '*Sun Lunch*', 'Church Vest-
ments', 'Obituary Notices', 'Undertakers'

Chapter XXI

Dick meets a strange American who, it seems, sells U.S. newspapers
and is determined to get his share of all the money that is coming into
Europe with the rich Americans. He finally shakes the man off and
realises that he has missed Rosemary. He telephones her at the hotel
and tells her that he wants to be with her. Rosemary continues to write
a letter to her mother in which she speaks of her latest director and
suggests that they should leave for Hollywood. Dick telephones Nicole
and they go to a play, following their belief that they should never
allow themselves to feel too tired for anything.

NOTES AND GLOSSARY:

Cheyne-Stokes: a form of breathing with a cyclical variation in the rate which becomes slower until breathing stops for several seconds before speeding up to a climax and then slowing once more. This occurs when sensitivity of the respiratory centre in the brain is impaired

Otard. . . . Armagnac: brandy or cognac

Chapter XXII

Nicole wakes to find a *sergent de ville* at her door looking for Abe North. He explains that Abe North is in Paris and has been robbed by a Negro whom they believe they now have under arrest. Nicole finds out that Abe has registered at the hotel and receives a call from the hotel office which tells her that a Negro downstairs wishes to speak to her; this man is a friend of the Negro under arrest, Mr Freeman, and wishes to appeal for help to avert an injustice. Nicole says that they know nothing about it.

Rosemary and Nicole go shopping together and to their pleasure find Dick back at the hotel on their return. He tells of a strange series of telephone calls, one from Abe in which the latter had claimed to have started a race riot in Montmartre and intended to release Freeman from his arrest. When he had given Dick an absurd answer as to why he was back in Paris, Dick had hung up. Nicole tells Rosemary how nice Abe was when they first knew him, implying an unfavourable comparison with the present. She comments on how many 'smart men go to pieces nowadays', which annoys Dick. They lunch together and notice a group of 'gold-star' mothers who have lost sons in the war. This triggers off nostalgic childhood memories in Dick, but then he turns his thoughts back to the world around him.

NOTES AND GLOSSARY:

sergent de ville :   police constable

Fernand: possibly referring to Fernand Léger (1881–1955), a French painter famous for his machine-like images and modern or futuristic settings

gold-star muzzers: gold star mothers. The episode is a testament to Dick Diver's sentimentality and nostalgia for the past. Gold-star mothers were those whose sons had been killed in the First World War

---

Chapter XXIII

Abe North is in the Ritz bar and talks to Paul, the concessionaire. He enjoys prolonging this bout of irresponsible behaviour. At four, having spent all day in the bar, he is asked if he wants to see another Negro, Jules Peterson. Peterson is not allowed to enter the hotel bar, so Abe goes out to meet him.

NOTES AND GLOSSARY:
Liberty: an American magazine

Chapter XXIV

Dick Diver thinks of ;{osemary and Nicole with consternation as he carries out various personal errands. He goes to Rosemary's hotel room; they kiss, but Dick is haunted by the thought of his responsibilities to Nicole. There is a knock at the door which startles them, but it proves only to be Abe North. With him is Jules Peterson; they request Dick's help and they all go over to the Divers' suite. Jules Peterson had witnessed the robbery in Montparnasse and later had incorrectly identified a Negro as the criminal. The police had then arrested Freeman, a negro restauranteur, for no apparent reason. Peterson is now in trouble for betraying fellow Negroes and wants protection, which Abe has promised, in the form of financial aid and help with his business. Dick tells Abe that he should go to bed and suggests that Peterson should go and see Abe when he is in better shape. Peterson offers to wait in the hall to allow Dick and Abe to talk in private. When Abe finally leaves in a pathetic state he finds to his relief that Peterson is no longer in the corridor.

NOTES AND GLOSSARY:
arrondissement: (*French*) a district of the city, one of the twenty wards in Paris
anagrams: a game in which words are made by rearranging the letters of other words or by arranging letters taken at random

---

Chapter XXV

Dick and Rosemary embrace before Rosemary returns to her room. Gradually she realises that she is not alone: the body of Peterson is lying on her bed. In panic she fetches Dick, who confirms that he is dead. There is blood on the bedclothes, and Dick asks Nicole to bring some clean bedclothes from their room, for Dick quickly realises that it is essential for Rosemary's career that she is not connected with this murder. He drags the body into the corridor, then reports that they have found a body to the hotel's manager-owner, McBeth, requesting complete confidentiality in dealing with the police.

When Dick returns to his room he learns from Rosemary that Nicole is in the bathroom. To Rosemary's surprise, he rushes anxiously to see her. At first Rosemary thinks Nicole must be hurt, but then she glimpses Nicole kneeling beside the bath, swaying and screaming incoherently about a bedspread with red blood on it and accusing Dick of intruding on her only sanctuary, the bathroom. Rosemary withdraws, greatly shaken, now understanding what it was that Violet McKisco had seen at Villa Diana. At that moment the telephone rings and she is greatly relieved to find that it is Collis Clay.

NOTES AND GLOSSARY:
couverture: (*French*) a coverlet or blanket
Arbuckle: Roscoe 'Fatty' Arbuckle (1887–1933), an American comic actor, director and screenwriter. His career was ruined by scandal in 1921. At a drinking party a starlet named Virginia Rappe was seized by severe convulsions after supposedly having been sexually assaulted by him. She died a few days later and Arbuckle was charged with manslaughter. The case was tried several times, and Arbuckle was ultimately acquitted but his films were banned and his career essentially ended

BOOK TWO

Chapter I

Dr Richard Diver arrived in Zurich in 1917, aged twenty-six. He had gone to Oxford as a Rhodes Scholar in 1914, and in the next year had taken his degree at Johns Hopkins University. In 1916 he had gone to Vienna to arrive there, he hoped, before Freud became a casualty of the war. This was the heroic period in Dick Diver's life. In Vienna, he lived with Ed Elkins, the second secretary at the American Embassy, and it was Elkins who had first made him question the extent of his intelligence.

Dick was ordered to join a neurological unit at Bar-sur-Aube and there completed his textbook. After he was discharged, he returned to Zurich in 1919.

NOTES AND GLOSSARY:
illusions of a nation . . . cabin door: America and the American Dream. Dick Diver is the perfect representative of this dream, as was another Fitzgerald hero, Jay Gatsby, in *The Great Gatsby*. Thus Dick Diver's subsequent shedding of illusions has a wider significance and application to the nation as a whole

the hero, like Grant...Galena: General Ulysses S. Grant (1822–85) served in the war against Mexico but later resigned his commission; he was known for drinking to excess. In 1860 he went to Galena, Illinois, where he worked as a clerk in his father's leather store, apparently a broken man. With the outbreak of the Civil War, however, he joined the Union forces and was so successful that he became their supreme commander, and, later, the President of the United States (1868–76)

Chapter II

It is April and Dick has decided to stay in Zurich for two more years. He visits Franz Gregorovious at Dohmler's clinic on the Zurichsee where Franz is the resident pathologist. They discuss a patient, a girl whom Dick had met once before. She had been so taken with Captain Diver that she had written him about fifty letters over a period of eight months. Some letters showed a pathological problem but others were perfectly normal, and from this correspondence Dick has come to understand much of what is troubling Nicole Warren. Franz begins to tell Dick the girl's story.

NOTES AND GLOSSARY:

a Vaudois: or Waldenses, a Christian sect in southern France in the twelfth century. The name comes from Peter Waldo, a twelfth-century French heretic. The group adopted Calvinist ideas in the sixteenth century

Cagliostro: Count Alessandro di Cagliostro (1743–95), an Italian alchemist and imposter

Kraepelin: Emil Kraepelin (1856–1926), who contributed to psychiatry and to the classification of the abnormal states it dealt with. Kraepelin actually developed one theory of schizophrenia, which is of interest in the light of Nicole Warren's illness

plus petite...: (*French*) 'smaller and less intelligent'

Michigan Boulevard: a main thoroughfare in Chicago

Chapter III

Doctor Dohmler had corresponded with an American in Lausanne named Devereux Warren, of the Warren family of Chicago. Warren had brought his sixteen-year-old daughter Nicole to the clinic and had a consultation about her with Dohmler. He had explained that Nicole's mother had died when she was eleven. Nicole had been normal until some months ago, when he had had to dismiss a valet after she claimed that the man had made advances to her, and although these allegations turned out to be untrue, Nicole had continued to have ideas about being attacked. Dohmler had felt that something was wrong with Warren's story and Nicole was diagnosed as having a split personality. When Dohmler finally got Warren back for a second visit, the truth was revealed: Warren had been extremely close to his daughter after his wife's death and suddenly they had become lovers. It had happened just once. Dohmler thought the man a peasant and had suggested that he should go home to Chicago.

NOTES AND GLOSSARY:
un homme très chic: (*French*) 'a very elegant man'

Chapter IV

Franz explains that the case was accepted on the condition that Warren should not see his daughter for at least five years. Franz says that Dick's letters helped Nicole, but she had never discussed what had happened. He asks Dick to be gentle with her when he sees her. They discuss Dick's plans and Dick has dinner with Franz and his wife. Dick feels that Switzerland suits him as he has been treated too well elsewhere, and that is not good for a 'serious' man. He is coming to terms with his idealism and realises that he had wanted to be good, kind, brave, wise and also loved, but that that is difficult to achieve.

NOTES AND GLOSSARY:
the Gross-Münster: the cathedral in Zurich
Zwingli: Huldreich or Ulrich Zwingli (1484–1531), the Swiss Reformation leader
Heinrich Pestalozzi: Johann Heinrich Pestalozzi (1746–1827), Swiss educationalist
he wanted . . . loved, too: this shows Dick Diver as a compulsive giver, something that finally eats up all his resources and shows that morality can be a weakness. This formula is one Dick repeats throughout the novel

Chapter V

Nicole Warren comes to meet Dick accompanied by another woman. Nicole and Dick discuss their plans and Dick is impressed by her youth and beauty. She goes for a brief walk with Dick and promises to play records for him on his next visit. He comes a week later and finds himself increasingly attracted to her.

NOTES AND GLOSSARY:
Muy bella: (*Spanish*) 'very beautiful'
Buenas noches: (*Spanish*) 'Good-night'

Chapter VI

Dick sees Nicole again in May and they have lunch together. He would like to see Nicole independently happy and confident but realises that she worships him. In Zurich, Dick prepares to revise his *A Psychology for Psychiatrists*, a subject which he tells Franz he feels he will never understand any better than he does now. Franz believes that Dick will soon write books so simple that they will not give cause for thought. Franz also tells Dick that Nicole is in love with him and that they must be careful. Doctor Dohmler tells Dick that the so-called 'transference' must end as Nicole would not survive rejection by Dick. Dick finally admits he is a little in love with her and has considered marriage. Franz warns him of the dangers of devoting the rest of his life to being her doctor.

NOTES AND GLOSSARY:
St Hilda's: one of the women's colleges of Oxford University
Du lieber...:   (*German*) 'Dear God! Please bring Dick another glass of beer.'
transference: the redirection towards the psychiatrist of the patient's feelings and desires, especially those unconsciously retained from childhood

---

Chapter VII

It is decided that Dick must be kind to Nicole but must end his own emotional involvement. He meets Nicole at the main entrance of the clinic and she tells him of her most recent plans. Dick tells Nicole that she will be happy, but notices how much she desires his approval. He tells her that she must forget the past and go home to America to fall in love. He tactlessly mentions her illness and Nicole remarks that she knows she would not be fit to marry for a while. She is shattered by his attitude. Dick decides to complete the break in their relationship after supper. However, Nicole asks to be excused that evening, and Dick learns from Franz that he thinks she has understood his intentions.

NOTES AND GLOSSARY:
burberry: raincoat
Bonjour...:   (*French*) 'Good-day, Doctor.' 'Good-day, Monsieur.' 'The weather's good.' 'Yes, marvellous.' 'You are here now?' 'No, only for the day.' 'Ah, good. Well—good-bye, Monsieur.'

Chapter VIII

Dick reflects that Nicole's emotions had been poorly treated and he is haunted by her in his dreams. Once, he catches a glimpse of her in a Rolls Royce.

He arrives in Montreux on a cycling trip and boards the Glion funicular. In the cable car he meets the Conte de Marmora and Nicole. She too is going to Caux and seems happy and well. Nicole asks Dick to dinner and introduces him to her sister. Dick is conscious of Nicole's love for him as he leaves.

NOTES AND GLOSSARY:

Necessarily ... awhile: see Shakespeare, Hamlet (V, ii, 338–41): 'If thou didst ever hold me in thy heart,/ Absent thee from felicity awhile,/ And in this harsh world draw thy breath in pain,/ To tell my story.'

funicular: a cable railway ascending a mountain. The ascending car counterbalances a descending car

Défense ... : (*French*) 'It is forbidden to pick the flowers'

Irene Castle: an American dancer (1893–1969) who performed with her husband Vernon Castle. She was the first prominent personality to bob her hair and began the fashion

Chapter IX

Dick finds Miss Warren, Nicole and Marmora waiting for him at the hotel, and they are joined by Marmora's parents. Baby Warren tells Dick that she is aware that he has helped Nicole to get well. She confides that she is still worried about her sister and Dick finds that she does not know the real reason for Nicole's illness. She believes that the best thing for Nicole would be to meet and fall in love with a doctor. Dick is amused at the thought of the Warrens 'buying' Nicole a doctor.

Dick offers to go to find Nicole, who is missing. He discovers her outside, and she explains that she needed to get away. She asks him if he would have been interested in her if she had been well, and becomes angry when Dick ignores the question. She asks him to give her a chance, and they kiss. It starts to rain and they go back inside. Dick thinks of himself marrying a mental patient and concludes that the Warrens had better buy a doctor in Chicago. He receives a note from Nicole expressing no regrets, and another from her sister requesting him to accompany Nicole back to Zurich. He believes this to be purposeful planning on the part of Baby Warren, although this is not true.

The effect is what Dick has feared, for he feels totally involved with Nicole by the time he leaves her at the clinic.

NOTES AND GLOSSARY:
Vanity Fair: a magazine
Bull!:   (*slang*) 'Rubbish!'

Chapter X

In September, Dick has tea in Zurich with Baby Warren. She is against his marrying Nicole, since Nicole is rich and the family does not know anything about Dick. He explains that his father is a retired clergyman, that he comes from Buffalo, New York, and that he attended Yale. He tells her more, but Baby is not impressed.

Nicole's running monologue then encompasses the events of the next several years and her married life with Dick. She relates that Dick does not want any of her money, and thinks about her happiness in their love. There are references to his book, her pregnancies and their travels. Nicole has had two more attacks of insanity. She wants to have some kind of knowledge to keep her sane. They are on the Riviera, and the Norths are mentioned. She says that Tommy Barban is in love with her, and, on the beach, she sees Rosemary for the first time.

NOTES AND GLOSSARY:
Buffalo: in upstate New York
Mad Anthony Wayne: an American Revolutionary War general (1745–96)
Marshall Field: an American merchant (1834–1906) who founded Chicago's largest department store
Je m'en fiche de tout: (*French*) 'to hell with it all'
Mistinguette: Mistinguett (*sic*) was the stage name of Jeanne Marie Bourgeois (1874–1956), a popular French singer
Picasso: Pablo Picasso (1881–1973), the painter whose work has had a profound influence on modern art

Chapter XI

The narrative returns to the present. Dick and Elsie Speers are at the Café des Alliés. They discuss Rosemary. She tells him that Rosemary was sincere in her feelings for him and he admits that he loves her. Dick finds that he appreciates Mrs Speers's own charm.

At the Villa Diana, he reviews the material for his book. From the window he sees Nicole in the garden; he is depressed by the thought that henceforth he will always have to keep up a 'perfect front' with her. They had talked about Rosemary on the way home from Paris after Nicole's breakdown. He had criticised Rosemary but Nicole had praised her. He finds it hard to forget Rosemary. He is annoyed at Nicole for this latest attack of her illness and wonders whether he feels professional detachment or just a personal coldness towards her.

NOTES AND GLOSSARY:

wagon-lit :   (*French*) sleeping car
ceinture: (*French*) literally, 'belt'. Here it refers to the railway network, presumably of the inner urban area

Chapter XII

Dick finds Nicole in the garden and tells her that he has seen Mrs Speers. He has no wish to talk but wants to be alone so that he can concentrate on work and not on love. He plays the piano but stops as he realises that the tune will betray to Nicole his nostalgia for recent events. He thinks about the house and Nicole's money. He finds his work confused with the problems of Nicole, and that her money seems to belittle what he is doing; he does not feel free. In December, when Nicole seems well again, the Divers go to the Swiss Alps for the Christmas holidays.

NOTES AND GLOSSARY:

Sigmund Freud: the Austrian neurologist and founder of psychoanalysis (1856–1939)
Ward McAllister: a prominent leader of society in New York City, who originated the expression used to define the inner circle of society, 'the Four Hundred'. In 1892 he was asked by Mrs William Astor to help her reduce the guest list to her annual ball to four hundred, and McAllister later remarked that there were really only four hundred people in New York who could be considered members of society
mistral: a strong, cold northerly wind prevalent in winter and spring in Mediterranean countries
Syndicat d'Initiative : tourist board

Chapter XIII

Baby Warren joins the Divers at Gstaad. She is beginning to act like a spinster. Nicole urges Dick to dance with the young girls, but Dick rejects the idea. He meets Franz Gregorovious who suggests that they become partners in a clinic on the Zugersee. Baby says that they must think this over carefully but Dick resents her interference, for he feels it implies that the Warrens now own him. Later, he agrees to try the scheme with Franz.

NOTES AND GLOSSARY:

Sturmtruppen: (*German*) storm troops, trained to make the initial assault in battle. Here it is of course an amusingly exaggerated metaphor

Privatdocent: an unsalaried university professor. It should be spelt *Privatdozent*

Jung...Bleuler...Forel...Adler: psychiatrists. Carl Gustav Jung (1875–1961), Eugen Bleuler (1857–1939) and August Henri Forel (1848–1931) were Swiss; Alfred Adler (1870–1937) was Austrian

Wiener: Viennese

Chapter XIV

Dick awakes from a dream of 'non-combatant's shell-shock'. They have been at the clinic for a year and a half. It has all seemed wasted time for Nicole, who has led a lonely life, 'owning' Dick against his will. Dick's son, Lanier, comes in to watch his father shave and Dick goes up to the administrative building. He is thirty-eight. He begins his rounds and speaks with a few patients. His most interesting patient is a woman of thirty who has developed nervous eczema. Dick feels close to her and wants to help her in her pain. He visits a young neurotic girl of fifteen and a sick psychiatrist, and then goes to lunch.

NOTES AND GLOSSARY:

Pyrrhic victory: a victory achieved at too great a cost. Pyrrhus, king of Epirus, defeated the Romans at Asculum (279 BC) but the battle left his forces depleted and exhausted

Chapter XV

After lunch, Dick returns to the villa to find Nicole with a letter which accuses him of seducing the daughter of a patient. He tells Nicole that the writer is deranged and the accusation totally groundless but she does not believe him. They take the children on an outing to the fair. At the fair, Nicole runs away and Dick finds her laughing hysterically in a car on top of a ferris wheel. She explodes into further wild statements, but then breaks down and asks for Dick's help. They leave and Dick is convinced that Nicole must help herself. On a hill, Nicole grabs the steering wheel and the car swerves off the road into a tree. Nicole is laughing and says that he was scared because he wanted to live. Dick feels only disgust for her.

NOTES AND GLOSSARY:

guignol:	see note on p.27
Hootchy-kootchy:	a dance
est-ce que . . . :	(*French*) 'May I leave these little ones with you for a couple of minutes? It's very urgent—I'll give you ten francs.' 'Certainly.'
Alors—restez. . . :	(*French*) 'Stay with this kind lady.'
buvette:	(*French*) refreshment tent
La septième . . . :	(*French*) 'The seventh daughter of a seventh daughter born on the banks of the Nile—come in, Monsieur—'
Plaisance:	(*French*) place of amusement
Regardez . . . :	(*French*) 'Look at that!' 'Look at that English-woman!'
Svengali:	a mesmerist able to control his subject's actions. Svengali is a character in the novel *Trilby* (1894) by George du Maurier (1834–96)
corium:	or cutis; the deepest layer of the skin
Merci . . . :	(*French*) 'Thank you, Monsieur, ah Monsieur is too generous. It was a pleasure, Monsieur, Madame. Good-bye, my little ones.'
La voiture . . . :	(*French*) 'The Divers' car is broken.'

Chapter XVI

Dick tells Franz that he wishes to go away for at least a month. This last episode with Nicole has been too much for him. The following week he leaves for Munich. Over the Vorarlberg Alps, Dick lets his imagination wander and he thinks of life in the villages below. He thinks, too, of his boyhood. He still keeps a hold on his intelligence.

NOTES AND GLOSSARY:
dementia praecox: a form of insanity

Chapter XVII

Dick meets Tommy Barban in Munich and Tommy introduces him to Prince Chillicheff, Mr McKibben and Mr Hannan. It seems that Tommy and the Prince have just come from Russia. The Prince had been in hiding and Tommy helped him to escape. McKibben offers Dick a ride to Innsbruck, which he refuses. During the conversation Tommy mentions a murder in a speak-easy, and it emerges that Abe North has been beaten to death in a speak-easy in New York. Dick is stunned by the news and feels much regret for his own lost youth.

NOTES AND GLOSSARY:

speak-easy: Prohibition in the United States, which began in 1920, meant the outlawing of alcoholic beverages. Bootlegging sprang up to bring in illegal alcohol and speak-easies replaced saloons to sell the illegal alcohol. Prohibition was repealed in 1933

Chapter XVIII

At Innsbruck, Dick thinks of Nicole and how he loves her when she is at her best. He feels that he has lost confidence in himself because of his association with the Warren money. He believes, however, that he is not yet defeated by the rich. He feels in love with every pretty woman he sees; there is one woman in particular, but he resists.

There is a cable from Buffalo telling him of his father's death. He is sad that his father has died alone, and thinks how he was always guided morally by him. He arranges to go to America for the funeral.

NOTES AND GLOSSARY:
Erbsen-suppe: (*German*) pea soup
Würstchen: (*German*) sausages
Helles **of Pilsener**: a light-coloured beer
Kaiserschmarren: (*German*) literally, 'Emperor pancakes'

Chapter XIX

Dick takes his father's body to Virginia to be buried alongside other relatives, and believes that he will never return again. He wishes good-bye to his father and to all his ancestors.

On the steamship on the way back he meets Albert McKisco. McKisco is now a successful author and Dick is glad to talk to him. Dick goes on to Naples, entertains a family from the ship, and goes to Rome the next day. He meets Rosemary in the hotel; she is in Rome making a film and tells him to call her later. He thinks of the past, and the fact that he is older. On his way to see her, he meets Collis Clay, who informs him that Rosemary is now an experienced woman.

NOTES AND GLOSSARY:
couturières: (*French*) fashion designers, dress-makers
Corriere della Sera: one of the major Italian newspapers
una novella...: (*Italian*) 'a novel by Sainclair Lewis, *Wall Street*, in which the author analyses the social life of a small American town'. The newspaper is a little inaccurate: the writer's name was Sinclair Lewis (1885–1951) and the novel *Main Street* (1920)

Chapter XX

Dick finds Rosemary in black pyjamas and compliments her on her beauty. She mentions her mother. The phone keeps interrupting them but finally they kiss. Later, he tries making love to Rosemary but eventually she declines. Dick wants to know the truth about her and does not believe her when she suggests that her experiences with love have been abortive. They go for a walk and Rosemary promises to take him to the set in the film studios the next day.

Dick is shown around the set the next day, finding it chaotic and turbulent. They have lunch and, back at the hotel, they make love.

NOTES AND GLOSSARY:

Edna Ferber:	an American novelist and dramatist (1885–1968) whose works include *Show Boat* (1926), *Saratoga Trunk*, and *Dinner at Eight*
the Junior Prom:	a spring dance held in the third year of secondary school in America
hopeful Valentinos:	actors ambitious to emulate the success of Rudolph Valentino (1895–1926), a famous star of silent films

Chapter XXI

Dick drinks a cocktail with Collis Clay and realises he is being self-indulgent about Rosemary. He runs into Baby Warren and they have dinner together. They discuss Nicole, and Collis Clay joins them. Baby suggests that if Nicole would be happier with someone other than Dick, it could be arranged. None the less, the Warrens are grateful to him for what he has done for Nicole. Dick tries asking Baby about herself; he admires her and compliments her.

Dick has lunch with Rosemary the next day. He realises that neither of them are in love, though he feels passion for her. Again, he asks her about her past. They argue over her relationship with her leading man, Nicotera. Dick is jealous and Rosemary is confused. Nicotera wants to marry her. Dick decides to leave and Rosemary tells him she does not care for Nicotera but must leave Rome with the company the next morning. She says she will stay with him that evening, but Dick retreats and they say good-bye. He remarks that he is no longer able to make people happy and is like the Black Death.

NOTES AND GLOSSARY:

Michael Arlen:	a British novelist (1895–1956) whose work mirrored the London high-life of the 1920s. His best-known novel was *The Green Hat* (1924)

| adagio: | a piece of music in slow time |
| the Black Death: | the great plague which ravaged Europe in the fourteenth century |

Chapter XXII

Dick is with Collis Clay at the Quirinal bar, complaining about the Italians. He receives a note from Rosemary which tells him she is in her room, but Dick instructs the bell-boy to tell her that he cannot be found. He and Collis go to a cabaret at the Bonbonieri and continue to drink. Dick has an argument with the orchestra leader. He meets an English girl who promises to come over and join them later. He argues with Collis, but all is well between them when Collis departs. Dick dances with the girl, who suddenly disappears. He leaves and has a dispute over a taxi fare with four drivers. A fight begins and they go to the police station to settle the matter. The Captain tells Dick he must pay the fare requested and Dick angrily hits the man who has brought him to the station. In turn, he is badly beaten. He had hit a plain-clothes lieutenant. As Dick is dragged into a cell, he yells to one of the taxi-drivers to contact Miss Warren at the Excelsior Hotel.

NOTES AND GLOSSARY:

Quanto . . . :	(*Italian*) 'How much to the Quirinal Hotel?' 'A hundred lira.' . . . 'Thirty-five lira and the tip.' 'A hundred lira.'
carabinieri :	military policemen
Alors . . . :	(*French*) 'Then listen. Go to the Quirinal. You zombie! Listen: you're drunk. Pay what the taxi-driver asks for. Do you understand?' . . . 'No, I won't.' 'What?' 'I'll pay forty lira. It's quite enough.' . . . 'Listen! You're drunk. You hit the taxi-driver. Like this! It's a good thing I'm letting you go. Pay what he said—a hundred lira. Go to the Quirinal.'
due centi lire :	(*Italian*) Two hundred lira

Chapter XXIII

The concierge wakes Baby Warren at four in the morning and informs her that Dick is in trouble with the police. Baby takes a taxi to the police station and from an archway hears Dick screaming and shouting. He insists that they have put his eye out and beaten him. Baby tries to get some action from the guards but, failing to do so, goes to the American Embassy. At the Embassy she receives little help from a young man with his face covered with pink cold cream and wearing a white embroidered Persian robe. Despite Baby's vociferous protests she is directed to the American consulate. She enlists the aid of Collis Clay and they both go back to the jail. Collis stays with Dick, and Baby goes to the consulate to see the Consul. She is made to wait until finally she pushes into his office and orders him to help. At last he contacts a vice-consul.

Dick becomes aware of his great irresponsibility and the effects of what has happened. The vice-consul, Swanson, arrives and they go to court. Dick is disturbed by hissing and booing from the crowd as he crosses the courtyard. The people have mistaken him for a criminal charged with the rape and murder of a five-year-old child. Dick is freed, but exclaims that he wants to explain to the crowd how he raped the child. Baby waits with a doctor in the taxi. She is satisfied in knowing that the Warrens now possess moral superiority over Dick for as long as they need him.

NOTES AND GLOSSARY:
Non capisco inglese: (*Italian*) 'I don't understand English.'
Bene: (*Italian*) 'Well'
But he was ... too hard for her: the east coast of the United States, in particular the northeast New York–Boston area, is alluded to here. As a Chicagoan, Baby Warren would be at a distinct disadvantage, or so Fitzgerald would seem to suggest. The northeast population considered itself more sophisticated than people in other parts of the country—an attitude which some would interpret as effete snobbery
semper dritte...: (*Italian*) 'straight on, right ... left'

BOOK THREE

Chapter I

Frau Kaethe Gregorovious tells her husband that she and Nicole do not get on. She suggests that Nicole is not really so ill and that Dick married her for her money. After Dick's return from Rome, she mentions that she believes Dick has been on a debauch. She contends that he is no longer a 'serious' man. Franz defends him, but, in the end he is also convinced of these changes in Dick.

NOTES AND GLOSSARY:
Birds in their little nests agree: a line from one of the *Divine and Moral Songs for Children* by Isaac Watts (1674–1748), an English hymn writer
Norma Talmadge: an American actress (1893–1957)

Chapter II

Dick gives Nicole an untruthful version, more favourable to himself, of what happened in Rome and throws himself into his work to get over the episode. Franz finds an opportunity to start the break with Dick: he sends him on a case to Lausanne to help a father with an alcoholic homosexual son. Dick tells Señor Pardo y Ciudad Real that they can only help his son with his alcoholism, and he interviews the boy. To his surprise he meets Royal Dumphry, who is obviously a homosexual friend of the boy. Dumphry reminds Dick of the dinner he had once enjoyed at the Divers' on the Riviera and then tells Dick that Nicole's father, Devereux Warren, is dying in Lausanne. Dick contacts the doctor on the case and is informed that Warren wants to see his daughter. Dick visits Devereux Warren and promises to consult his associate about a possible visit from Nicole. Dick telephones the clinic and asks Kaethe to pass on his message to Franz. Although Kaethe does not intend to tell Nicole, she ends up by giving her the news about her father, and Nicole immediately takes the train to Lausanne. Meanwhile, Dick learns the incredible news that Warren has recovered enough to leave Lausanne. He attempts to catch up with Warren at the station but without success. Nicole is puzzled to learn that her father has gone.

NOTES AND GLOSSARY:

Wassermanns: tests for syphilis, a venereal disease
Harrow: an English public school
cantharides: a preparation with aphrodisiac properties
bordello: brothel
it was as if . . . complete themselves: this emphasises what has happened to Dick Diver as a result of his constant giving. His life and self have become defined by what he has given to other people, to such an extent that he has not got an independent self. He *is* those people and cannot stand alone
persona grata: (*Latin*) an acceptable person
'The Wedding of the Painted Doll': a popular song from *Babes in Toyland* by Victor Herbert (1859–1924)

Chapter III

A week later, a patient at the clinic, Von Cohn Morris, and his parents are putting his luggage into a limousine. Dick Diver talks to the father and is told that the son is being taken away because of Dick's drinking. Dick is shaken by this charge and writes out a programme intended to reduce his drinking. Franz returns from a holiday and Dick tells him what has happened. Franz suggests 'a leave of abstinence', or 'absence' as Dick corrects him. Franz believes Dick's heart is no longer in the project and Dick says he wants to leave. Dick is unprepared for Franz's quick agreement with this idea, but is also relieved.

NOTES AND GLOSSARY:

duster: a lightweight coat

vin du pays: (*French*) the local wine

Chapter IV

The Divers decide to return to the Riviera. They travel around before their return and Dick gets to know the children better. They have plenty of money now and travel in grand style. In Italy they visit Mary North, now the Contessa di Minghetti. This is a papal title and Mary's husband owns manganese deposits in south-west Asia.

Nicole mentions to Dick that one of two children by a previous marriage of the Count is ill and that the children should be warned to keep away from him. Dick talks to the Count, Hosain, and tells him preposterous stories about the grandeur of Hollywood. The next day Lanier complains of being made to take a bath in the dirty water used by the sick boy. Dick explains to one of the Asiatic women that his children must not be bathed in the sick boy's water, and upsets her. At dinner, Hosain leaves early and later Mary receives a note informing her that her husband is going on a brief journey.

Mary confronts the Divers the following morning and asks why her husband's sister had been told to clean a bath. The Divers are amazed —they had thought that the woman was a servant. Mary explains that Hosain has left the house to protect his honour. Lanier is questioned about the incident, despite Nicole's objections. Finally Mary says they must stay, for it was just a misunderstanding. Dick insults Mary, however, and the Divers leave.

NOTES AND GLOSSARY:

Newark: a city and port in northeast New Jersey

not quite light enough ... Mason-Dixon: Charles Mason and Jeremiah Dixon surveyed this boundary line between Maryland and Pennsylvania to a point about 244 miles west of the Delaware river between 1763 and 1767. The term 'Mason and Dixon Line' then came into popular use to designate the boundary between the free states and the slave states before the Civil War. A Pullman was a first-class railway coach and in the south Negroes were not allowed to travel in them

| major-domo: | the chief servant, managing the household |
| smoke: | a derogatory slang term for a Negro |

Chapter V

Nicole sees Dick arguing with the cook, Augustine, over her drinking their best wine. The cook threatens Dick with a butcher's knife and hatchet. Nicole suggests he give her extra money to leave and this settles the affair. The Divers go to Nice for dinner and Nicole remarks that they cannot go on as they have been doing; she thinks that she has ruined Dick.

Dick suggests that they should go out to the motor yacht of T.F. Golding in the Nicean bay. Nicole sees Tommy Barban on the yacht. She notices Lady Caroline Sibly-Biers, whom Tommy describes as the wickedest woman in London. In the dining salon, Dick sits next to Lady Caroline and offends her by insulting the English. There is a further scene between them and Nicole is furious at both. She looks for Dick later; he suggests that they are both ruined, and pulls her over as if he is going to have both of them commit suicide by jumping overboard. Instead, he lets her go, and Tommy appears. Tommy tells Nicole she should tell Dick not to drink, and, when the yacht arrives in Cannes, he drives the Divers home.

NOTES AND GLOSSARY:

poste de police:	(*French*) police station
Salud:	(*French slang*) a strong term of abuse (normally spelled *salaud*)
Bonne chance:	(*French*) 'good luck'
Mais pour nous héros...:	(*French*) 'But we heroes need time, Nicole. We can't do little exercises in heroism—we have to make grand compositions'
Parlez français...:	(*French*) 'Talk French with me, Nicole'
Ronald Colman:	a British film actor (1891–1958)
chemin-de-fer:	(*French*) a card game
John Held:	an American artist (1889–1958) of the twenties, cartoonist of flappers and the Jazz Age
Danny Deever:	a reference to a ballad of the same title by Rudyard Kipling (1865–1936)
Sepoys:	natives of India employed as soldiers by a European power
Quelle enfanterie...:	(*French*) 'What childishness!' 'You'd think he was reciting Racine!' (i.e. reciting from the plays of the classical French dramatist, Jean Racine, 1639–99)

Chapter VI

Dick goes into Nicole's room the next morning and asks her to forget the previous evening. Tommy asks after Nicole and Dick becomes defensive. Nicole knows that she dislikes Dick and that Tommy is in love with her. In her garden, she considers why she should have a lover and overhears a conversation between two men passing by who are discussing an affair of passion. She gives Tommy a special jar of camphor rub for his throat as he departs. Dick objects and later rejects her approaches to him. In June, when Tommy is in Nice, he writes to them. Dick also receives a telegram from Rosemary.

NOTES AND GLOSSARY:

distaff: part of a spinning wheel; hence a symbol of women's traditional role in the home

Chapter VII

Nicole goes to the beach with Dick the following day, worried that he will do something desperate. She fears the break with him, but not what will follow. She sees Dick looking for his children for his own protection. She realises that he might fear appearing on the beach he had once made fashionable, and is momentarily sorry for him. She stops feeling sorry as she sees him looking around for Rosemary.

Nicole sees Rosemary in the water, and the Divers swim out to greet her. Nicole watches the flattery begin and sees Dick's mood improve. Dick suggests that they join Rosemary's friends on a speedboat and Nicole wonders if he will make a spectacle of himself. The others perform stunts on the aquaplane and then Dick tries his 'lifting trick', makes three attempts and fails. Nicole worries about his final attempt, but when they go to rescue him from the water her worry changes to contempt.

Rosemary tells Dick how good it is to see him and that she had heard he had changed. Dick says that this is true and only his manner remains the same. Mary North is also on the beach and comes over only to see Rosemary. After Mary leaves, Rosemary is surprised by Dick's bitterness about her. She recalls the unfavourable things she has heard about Dick. Dick begins a lecture on acting and emotional responses. It is more than Nicole can stand, and when Rosemary asks Topsy if she would like to be an actress, Nicole sharply remonstrates with her and announces that she is leaving. She relaxes as she drives away and reflects that she is almost independent of Dick now. She writes to Tommy Barban in Nice. That evening, she once more fears what is in Dick's mind and realises that she must think for herself. They have a peaceful dinner and Dick plays the piano. In the morning she finds a note from him saying that he has gone away for a few days. To her pleasure, Tommy Barban telephones to tell her that he is driving over to see her.

NOTES AND GLOSSARY:

aquaplane: a board towed behind a speedboat and ridden by a person standing on it

The manner . . . cracks: Dick is trying to tell Rosemary that he has indeed fallen apart or dissipated to the point of no return. His words show just how much he has been aware of his decline since the Rome episode. The unfortunate incidents of Book Three, such as the scene in the clinic over his drinking, his exchanges with Mary North and later Lady Caroline Sibly-Biers, and the aquaplane stunt, are merely confirmation of what Dick already knows

faits accomplis: (*French*) things already done

an Anita Loos heroine: Anita Loos (1893–1982) was the American author of *Gentleman Prefer Blondes* (1925)

Either you think . . . sterilise you: for Nicole this is an essential statement of independence from Dick. Nicole is at last discovering its truth. There is great irony here, for in many ways this is just what has happened to Dick, through Nicole, her money and the pursuit of the illusions of his youth

Chapter VIII

Nicole bathes and reviews her physical beauty. Tommy comes and she enjoys being worshipped again. Tommy asks her when she began to have 'white crook's eyes' and Nicole is offended until she realises that the remark means nothing. Tommy believes that Dick's problem is that she has too much money. For the first time she feels another person's influence other than Dick's. They kiss and drive towards Nice. They stop at a small shore hotel and make love.

Nicole recognises that things will be different from what she had expected. Tommy notices a noise below their window: two American sailors are fighting and a crowd has gathered. When they finally leave, there is still more activity and noise. Two girls ask Tommy and Nicole if they may wave goodbye to the departing sailors from their balcony, and they agree.

They have dinner in Monte Carlo and swim in the moonlight at Beaulieu. Nicole feels that all that Dick has taught her is falling away.

NOTES AND GLOSSARY:
Chanel Sixteen: a costly perfume
apéritifs: (*French*) an *apéritif* is a drink taken before a meal as an appetiser. Here used figuratively
Parle français: (*French*) 'Speak French'
poules: (*French slang*) girls, literally, 'hens'

Chapter IX

To Nicole's surprise, Dick returns home the next day. He explains that he wanted to find out if Rosemary had anything to offer now, but he finds she has still not grown up. Nicole tells him that she went dancing with Tommy but Dick does not want to know the details. Dick goes to the work-room and Tommy calls on the phone. He insists that Dick should be told that all is over between them. Something can be done. Nicole is satisfied with all this but feels some remorse about Dick. She goes to see Dick and puts her arm around his shoulder, but is rebuffed. He tells her he cannot do anything more for her: he is trying to save himself. She cries but fights back, and at last wins her freedom. Dick feels that the 'case' is now over and that he is free at last.

NOTES AND GLOSSARY:
comment vas-tu?:   (*French*) 'how are you?'

Chapter X

At two in the morning Dick receives a call and delights in one more chance to be of use. The police are holding Mary North and Lady Caroline, who need to be bailed out for the sake of their reputations. The two women had dressed up as French sailors and had picked up two girls who made a scene when they realised the truth. One of the girls was of a respectable family and a settlement had to be made. Dick explains to the chief of police in outrageous terms that the two women are important and highly influential people. Later, old Gausse, the hotel owner, who has helped Dick with this matter and lent him the money for the settlement, kicks Lady Caroline when she refuses to pay the money she owes him.

NOTES AND GLOSSARY:
Oui, oui . . .:   (*French*) 'Yes, yes . . . but to whom am I speaking?'
pas de mortes . . .:   (*French*) 'not deaths, not cars'
Anglaise: (*French*) Englishwoman
fifty stripes of the cat: fifty lashes with a whip
cartes d'identité: (*French*) identity cards
landaulet: a motor-car with a removable top cover

John D. Rockefeller Mellon: Dick is being outrageous here. John D.
Rockefeller (1839–1937) was an American indus-
trialist who established Standard Oil and became
the world's richest person. Andrew W. Mellon
(1855–1937) was a financier and industrialist who
was the benefactor of the National Gallery of Art,
Washington, D.C.

Chapter XI

Dick and Nicole go for their customary haircuts. At the hairdresser's,
Nicole is surprised when Tommy Barban appears and walks into the
men's part of the shop. Tommy informs Dick that he wants to see him
and Dick pulls Nicole along, her hair still half cut, to the Café des
Alliés. Tommy explains that Nicole loves him and not Dick. Nicole
says she has grown fond of Tommy and that Dick does not care for her
any more. They are interrupted by an American selling newspapers and
Dick recognises him as the man he had encountered in Paris. Dick
states that he and Nicole have had much happiness together, but he is
distracted from the discussion by the Tour de France cycling race
coming through the town. The discussion continues and Dick decides
that the question has been settled. Tommy is slightly disappointed that
there has been no fight. Dick says he agrees in principle to a divorce
and will discuss things with Nicole. Tommy assumes the role of
Nicole's protector and admits that Dick has been fair. Nicole realises
that Dick had known what was to come ever since the camphor rub episode.

NOTES AND GLOSSARY:
coiffeuse: (*French*) hairdresser
citron pressé: (*French*) lemon juice
Il n'y a plus...:   (*French*) 'There's no more Black & White
                        [whisky]. We have only got Johnny Walker.' 'That
                        will do.'
Donnez moi...:   (*French*) 'Give me some gin with soda.'
Cessez cela...:   (*French*) 'Stop that! Clear off!'
allez-vouz-en: (*French*) 'Go away'
amour de famille: (*French*) family affection

Chapter XII

Dick Diver spends some time with his children before he leaves the
Riviera. He says goodbye to the staff at the Villa Diana, leaves a note
for Nicole and Baby Warren, and goes to look once more at the beach.

Nicole and her sister come on to the beach and Nicole sees Dick. Baby feels he should leave but Nicole argues that it is 'his' beach. She defends Dick. Dick sits with Mary Minghetti and drinks. Mary tells him it is his drinking that makes him unpleasant. Dick considers seducing Mary but abandons the idea when he begins to feel laughter inside himself. He has difficulty in standing up and Nicole wants to go to him but is restrained by Tommy.

NOTES AND GLOSSARY:

Doctor Eliot: Charles W. Eliot (1834–1926), an American educationist and President of Harvard University 1869–1909, remembered for his many reforms at Harvard. He helped to reform medical education with the aid of the author Dr Oliver Wendell Holmes (1809–94)

Chapter XIII

After her new marriage, Nicole still writes to Dick about business and the children. His office in Buffalo is unsuccessful and he moves several times. There is an unfortunate involvement with a girl and a lawsuit. Nicole's last word from Dick is from Hornell, New York, 'a very small town'.

Part 3

Commentary

Tender is the Night, Fitzgerald's philosophical or psychological novel, first appeared in April 1934. He had not published a novel since *The Great Gatsby* of 1925. Although he had a great commercial success with his first two novels, *This Side of Paradise* (1920) and *The Beautiful and Damned* (1922), he received little praise from critics for any of his work. *Tender is the Night* was characterised by Peter Quennell as 'a rather irritating type of chic'.* Dennis Harding gave it one of its rare good reviews in *Scrutiny*: 'The difficulty of making a convincing analysis of the painful quality of this novel, and the conviction that it was worthwhile trying to, are evidence of Scott Fitzgerald's skill and effectiveness.'†

These mixed reviews, and a general attitude taken by critics that Fitzgerald was not to be considered seriously, spurred Fitzgerald to revise *Tender is the Night*. He wrote: 'Its great fault is that the true beginning —the young psychiatrist in Switzerland—is tucked away in the middle of the book.' ** He came up with a new version in 1939 and this was published by Scribners in 1953 as the second of *Three Novels*. The events in the revised version are chronological. Instead of three books there are five, and instead of beginning with Rosemary Hoyt's arrival on the Riviera in June 1925, the novel begins with young Dick Diver in Vienna in 1917.

Themes

In *Tender is the Night* Fitzgerald has drawn a vivid picture of the Jazz Age and its superficial values. As in *The Great Gatsby*, he places these values within the context of reaching for the 'American Dream'. There is a confrontation between the solid values of Dick Diver's childhood in Buffalo, New York, where his father taught him about good instincts, courage, courtesy and honour (Book Two, ch. XVIII), and the power and wealth of the Warrens. There is also a pitting of the force of

---

* Quoted in *F. Scott Fitzgerald: A Collection of Critical Essays*, ed. Arthur Mizener, Prentice-Hall, Englewood Cliffs, New Jersey, 1963, p. 2.
‡ Dennis Harding, 'The mechanisms of failure', *Scrutiny*, III, December 1934.
** *The Letters of F. Scott Fitzgerald*, ed. Andrew Turnbull, Scribners, New York, 1963, p.281.

talent and imagination against the sheer weight of money. The character of the crude American selling newspapers underlines this power of American money. He shows Dick a newspaper clipping, a cartoon showing Americans in their millions disembarking from the liners with bags of gold: 'You think I'm not going to get part of that?' (Book Three, ch. XI).

Gone is hardy, moral, puritan America. The First World War of 1914–18 has provided the appropriate break with this past, and a decade of enormous prosperity has helped to erase the memory of the war. Occasionally there is a sentimental glimpse of life as it once was, as when Dick sees the gold-star mothers in Paris. He admires their unity and their dignity, and in these women sees 'the maturity of an older America.' For a moment he recalls his childhood days, then:

> Almost with an effort he turned back to his two women at the table and faced the whole new world in which he believed. (Book One, ch. 22)

This is Dick Diver's brave new world as it seemed to many young Americans with aspirations beyond their middle-class backgrounds. There is a sense here that one should be able to succeed—that money, love, youth and beauty are available. Furthermore, anyone with intelligence and ambition should be able to capture these things. Dick Diver, however, instead of capturing them, becomes controlled by them. Nicole possesses him first through her physical attractiveness and second through her wealth. His intellect and his dreams deteriorate throughout the novel. Nicole wants to own Dick and does not want him to succeed in his work. She 'encouraged any slackness on his part' (Book Two, ch. XII).

What Fitzgerald emphasises in *Tender is the Night* is what happens when one man's dreams meet what he thinks is their reality. It is both a romantic search and a seduction. Traditional, hard-working America has been taken in by a short cut to riches and success. Honest endeavour has been overcome by capitalist power. Fitzgerald makes the novel almost like a Marxist tract, but fills it with the reality of human failure. The theme is not tragic, merely impotent. Dick Diver does not die as his friend Abe North does, but suffers the worse fate of obscurity in small-town America: Nicole receives his latest correspondence from Hornell, New York.

On another level, Fitzgerald illustrates the issues of power and corruption, the users and those who are used. Nicole drains Dick Diver of both his moral strength and professional expertise. The Warrens are used to having people work for them, and to living on the labour of others: 'Nicole was the product of much ingenuity and toil' (Book One, ch. XII).

Even Nicole's own beauty and innocence have been tainted and corrupted by her incestuous relationship with her father. Rosemary is also corrupted, her innocence but another illusion of Dick Diver's. Dick allows himself to be used by both women—the one for strength while she is weak in illness, the other for simple entertainment. Dick's idealistic yearning to be a fine psychologist, perhaps the greatest of all, does not stand a chance when he is confronted with the opportunity to possess beauty, youth and the leisurely life which the possession of money permits. He simply loses his own freedom and the will to succeed, and he is destroyed by a superficial, materialistic, selfish society. The American Dream is either a total illusion or a sham. Power and corruption are inevitably linked and the simpler virtues crushed. The brutal power and force of Tommy Barban are the only answer to the monetary power and cool beauty of Nicole. There is nothing for Dick to do but go home.

Structure and technique

Fitzgerald's original version of the novel is constructed so that the events do not follow a chronological order but rather an impressionist order of time.* All the events are linked but, like a life reviewed in retrospect, the reader witnesses a sequence of those events that fit most closely together. This technique is appropriate for a 'psychological' novel because it makes the content of the events seem more significant than when they actually occur. It makes the impressions of individuals become the main factor that holds the novel together.

The narrator is the author, who writes his own continuous commentary throughout the simultaneous reflections of the other characters in the novel. This allows both for an omniscient voice and for the personal reactions of the characters involved. It permits us to compare these different views and examine the characters' different responses to the total story. Thus Fitzgerald has managed to frame this story by using the perspective of an external narrator yet maintaining an ability to focus closely on the lives, actions and reactions of its characters. Readers are given several points of view in turn by which to judge.

Book One presents the ambience of the French Riviera with its dazzling loveliness and wealthy, fashionable inhabitants. The first point of view Fitzgerald presents to us is that of Rosemary Hoyt, the young Hollywood film actress. The Riviera life is new to Rosemary and her eye scans its unfamiliar scenery like a camera exploring space. From her innocence and naïveté we first learn of the society of the beach, the

* See John F. Callahan, *The Illusions of a Nation: Myth and History in the Novels of F. Scott Fitzgerald*, University of Illinois Press, Urbana, 1972, p.63.

Divers and their realm. We are aware that there are two distinct groups on the beach and that the Divers' circle is somehow more refined and select. The McKiscos and Mrs Abrams, the homosexuals Dumphry and Campion, are simply not of the same social standing. Rosemary with her curious interest increasingly draws our attention to Dick Diver. Although we first see Dick as merely an image of carefree gaiety, it is quickly made clear that this man is the focal point of the whole society of the beach.

Thus, although the novel opens with Rosemary, an indication is given by her observations that Dick Diver is the main force, the protagonist of the novel. At the same time, the narration helps both to move the action along and to permit the reader to observe Rosemary. We immediately know what she looks like, who she is, and how much her mother Mrs Speers influences her in both thoughts and actions. Fitzgerald constantly uses a two-way mirror, a camera with two lenses, a system by which we look out from the inside and at the outside of his characters.

With each approximation to a camera shot Fitzgerald moves closer to the Divers. Rosemary meets them, is included in their society, and at last is invited to dinner. The big evening is arranged and grandly presided over by Dick. The Villa Diana is lovely and elegant, the company as varied as possible. Dr Diver is mischievously in control, pulling the two social groups of the beach together in a carefully orchestrated composition.

Dick Diver seems to control all; and the picture is too blissfully perfect. Rosemary is convinced of its wonderful quality and is totally unprepared for the scene that follows from her observations. Mrs McKisco has seen something awful in the bathroom and a series of events that break up this ideal setting quickly follow. However, although we have not been prepared by Rosemary for what happens, we have been prepared by the narration: the Divers' 'expensive simplicity' is 'part of a desperate bargain with the gods . . . attained through struggles she could not have guessed at' (Book One, ch. IV).

The fact that we start in the middle of the Divers's story and not the beginning leaves this situation a mystery, one which Fitzgerald can later build to an appropriate climax. It also allows the author slowly to strip away the veneer of this particular representation of the American Dream. All this wealth, beauty, youth and success still allows Violet McKisco to come across something dreadful in the bathroom. Furthermore, it causes a duel and leaves the final miserable scene of realisation in store for Rosemary.

Throughout the rest of Book One, we spiral down from an image of light-hearted perfection through a series of troubling episodes to the final grim truth about the Divers. The characters of their fine society decay around them and at last expose the Divers themselves. We react to Tommy Barban's cruel duel with Al McKisco, although, as it is anti-climactic, it seems an even more empty gesture. There is Abe North's obvious dissipation and the desperate scenes with him in Paris.

Throughout, Rosemary is there, seeing and trying to understand this brave new world. She is enamoured of its apparent leader, Dick Diver. The narration fills in what is not for Rosemary's eyes, piecing the story together. There is Rosemary's vain attempt to seduce Dick Diver and her fascination with Nicole's wealth and beauty. There is Dick's belated response to that attempt, a passion born out of learning that Rosemary is perhaps not totally innocent. From Dick Diver there is also a hint about Nicole's problems when he tells Rosemary that his relationship with Nicole is rather complex and that Nicole is not strong. Finally, Abe North, Dick's great partner in jokes, proves to have serious problems of his own. He tells Nicole that he is tired of them: 'If I had any enthusiasm, I'd go on to new people.... My business is to tear [things] apart.' (Book One, ch. XIX).

The narration has already given us a look at the character of Abe North from outside: from himself we get statements of his obvious unhappiness and distress. Abe North is another example of Dick Diver's fragmenting world. Once more, Fitzgerald uses Dick to try to pull it together. His positive influence and charm help the women to ignore Abe North's dissipation and the obvious flaw it represents in their idealistic world.

The story continues to move closer to Dick Diver. His abortive search for Rosemary in Passy shows him to be very human. We see him meet the more seamy side of an America of opportunities, in the character of the American selling newspapers, a man scarred and sinister.

Fitzgerald moves closer and closer to Dick's view, and away from Rosemary. We begin to realise that this is Dick's story and the narrative brings it all together. Dick acts and controls the others, Nicole, Rosemary and Abe. All the characters make this plain while the narrative builds up the background for conflict in Dick, facing 'the whole new world in which he believed'.

At the end of Book One Rosemary finally realises the truth about the Divers. After the episode with Abe North and Mr Peterson, the unfortunate Negro businessman, Peterson is murdered. The strain of the drama is too much for Nicole and she is found by both Dick and Rosemary, totally mad in the bathroom.

Book Two then explains what had gone wrong. From this alarming scene of Nicole raving and screaming, the reader is suddenly transported back to 1917 and the doctor, Richard Diver, aged twenty-six. The reader finds the crux of the novel here. The first book has brought us rapidly from a happy, carefree society to the terrible climax when the perfect girl of that society, Nicole Warren Diver, is suddenly totally shattered. From the narrative and the perspectives of various characters, we have had hints about her problems. Finally, with great dramatic emphasis, we are made to understand what Violet McKisco saw in the bathroom of the Villa Diana (Book One, ch. XXV).

We have almost come full circle. From this wretched scene, we are transported back to better times for Dick Diver in Zurich and Vienna. There is time to draw together more impressionist views. The First World War is seen from the safe island of Switzerland, as a blur of violence. Time blends with Dick's happy years of study at home and abroad. We are informed that this is his 'heroic period'. But Fitzgerald quickly shifts the scene to Dohmler's clinic on the Zurichsee in 1919. The case of a young girl, Nicole Warren, made ill as a result of an incestuous relationship with her father, is discussed. Fitzgerald holds our attention as he fills in this essential background from the point of view of Dick, the doctors and Nicole, as well as supplying a narration of events. Nicole's letters show her own attitude towards her illness and towards the young Captain Diver. The immediacy of these letters helps to make the retrospective world that Fitzgerald is reviewing more real. The reader is guided further into the past by the memory of Franz Gregorovious, who relates the meetings between Dr Dohmler and the father, Devereux Warren. This is all made up of snatches and impressions but the associative impact works. Book Two, which seems so different in tone from Book One, is more deeply connected and has greater impact because of the wealth of its explanatory background and the unexpected, climactic incident from which it sprang. Instead of Rosemary, Dick Diver now shares the main perspective with the narration. After the emotional drain at the end of Book One, this change is a welcome intermission and necessary device in order to ensure that what follows makes sense. The connecting or missing links offer us an opportunity to learn about Nicole's illness and background. We also learn about Dick Diver's original ambition: he tells Franz that he wants to be a very great psychologist.

The rest becomes something by which to measure just how much Dr Diver does or does not succeed. On the Riviera, in the first book, he has no role but that of leader and entertainer of a social set. Now it is revealed that he trained as a psychologist, and thus is a perfect companion for Nicole, whose beauty and wealth are flawed by corruption and insanity. Scene by scene Fitzgerald gives us a greater understanding of the situation. *Tender is the Night* is not a chronological study but one in which the psychological nuances are moulded together to create an overall impression of the characters.* The time itself is not the main

* See Callahan, *The Illusions of a Nation*, p.75.

element; what matters is the content of the events, as well as how these events fit in with each other. The narrative pulls us through this labyrinth and the perspectives of individual characters fill in more detail for greater impact.

Events move on. Nicole has fallen in love with the dashing Dr Diver. The other doctors suggest that he should end the relationship immediately. Diver agrees, but the narration lets us see into his personal reaction. Dick is not happy about the result: 'Nicole's emotions had been used unfairly—what if they turned out to have been his own?' (Book Two, ch. VIII).

Through what has happened in Book One, we already know what is imminent and inevitable. Dick Diver will marry Nicole, but why? In the narration, Fitzgerald has made it obvious that Nicole is physically attractive to Dick. Dick has admitted some emotion, to being half in love with Nicole, and that the question of marrying her had passed through his mind. He saw Nicole with a life which promised not just to be 'a projection of youth upon a greyer screen, but instead, a true growing' (Book Two, ch. VII).

Quickly, the scene switches yet again from the clinic to holidays in the Alps. Nicole is shown without a sign of illness in a mood of gaiety and normality, tinged only, perhaps, with an excessive vulnerability. Her sister, Baby Warren, is now introduced. Baby's viewpoint is added to the others and helps to explain much about Dick and Nicole. Baby makes an extraordinary statement to Dick. She informs him that their father has influence at the university in Chicago and suggests that perhaps they could place Nicole in with some university people: what could be better for her than to fall in love with a doctor?

This is a pivotal point and Dick, who both laughs at and is annoyed by the idea, finally becomes the doctor himself. But we are made clearly aware that Baby Warren finds the match unsuitable from the start, and the subsequent narrative confirms that her doubts are well founded.

Through Nicole's monologue in chapter X, Fitzgerald recounts the first years of her marriage to Dick. This technique is particularly effective, as was the use of Nicole's earlier letters to Captain Diver. We experience, with Nicole, the disorientation that goes with her schizophrenic condition. We are given factual information as well, such as that Dick Diver does not personally receive any of the Warren money. But most of all, we realise just how unstable Nicole is and how much of his time and devotion Dick has to put into bolstering her up.

As abruptly as we are taken from Nicole going mad at the end of Book One to young, idealistic Dick Diver in Zurich, we are swiftly brought back, in chapter XI, to the time directly after the Paris episode. Back at the Villa Diana, Dick Diver must face Nicole. With the reader now aware of Dick's professional and personal involvement, the narrative makes Dick's increasing dilemma evident. We are informed that he suffered 'unprofessional agonies' during her renewed illness after the birth of their second child. After this experience, Dick found it difficult 'to distinguish between his self-protective professional detachment and some new coldness in his heart' (Book Two, ch. XI).

We learn that Nicole's illness and her money are destroying Dick's peace of mind and his research. Her illness affects his work, but, in addition, her money, growing with the years, seems to make it of no consequence (Book Two, ch. VII). Fitzgerald is preparing us for another climax. This is now the story of Dick and Nicole. The narrative centres upon their struggle. The camera holds their lives in close-ups, always ensuring that it conveys an impression of their environments, from Gstaad to Cannes.

The Zugersee clinic provides yet another setting for the story and another shift in the plot. At last, Dick Diver, host of parties on the Riviera, is allowed an opportunity to resume his ambitions and his life's work. But Nicole and her sister Baby show how their attitudes continually weigh Dick Diver down in his attempts to achieve anything:

'Dick has me,' laughed Nicole. 'I should think that'd be enough mental disorder for one man' (Book Two, ch. XIII)

Franz Gregorovious has given Dick the opportunity to join him in running a clinic. Baby is quite interested in the idea, believing it to be in the best interests of her sister. She suggests they carefully review the offer. Dick is annoyed but responds mildly that it is nice of her to offer financial help but that the decision is for him to make, not her.

From this point, Fitzgerald puts into play a disastrous series of events. Nicole has a relapse, and causes an accident which could have been fatal. She mocks Dick and charges him with being frightened, declaring that Dick wanted to live (Book Two, ch. XV). It is too much for Dick, and the author now totally focuses on Dick by himself, away from Nicole and all the other pressures. The pressures, however, continue to follow him through a series of incidents. There is the reappearance of Tommy Barban in Munich, described as 'a ruler . . . a hero'. In the meeting with Tommy and his friends, Dick learns of Abe North's death in New York. He is told that Abe was beaten to death in a speak-easy (Book Two, ch. XVII). Dick's father dies in Buffalo and he has to go home for the funeral.

The rapid changes, the kaleidoscope of events that make up the second half of Book Two, do not stop there. Dick meets Rosemary in Rome. Fitzgerald makes us realise how much their outlooks, their attitudes have changed. Dick is now the one who adores and admires, but things are different. He recognises that at the age of eighteen, Rosemary could idolise a man of thirty-four, but that 'twenty-two would see thirty-eight with discerning clarity' (Book Two, ch. XIX).

Although the affair does begin again, Dick lacks enthusiasm for the relationship. It ends badly and quickly, leaving Dick Diver to remark finally: 'I'm the Black Death'. (Book Two, ch. XXI).

In what follows Dick Diver reaches the lowest point of his life. After a drunken dispute with some taxi-drivers, he finishes up beaten and broken in jail, only to be rescued by Baby Warren. The effects on him are too great to overcome. The narrative informs us that 'No mature Aryan is able to profit by a humiliation; when he forgives it has become part of his life' (Book Two, c. XXIII).

Fitzgerald has moved vivid scenes in and out to reach this miserable end quickly. Whereas in Book One Dick Diver is shown as strong and in control, through the misfortunes of other characters, in Book Two he is now the person destroyed and the Warren family has gained total control over him. What is left in Book Three is the verdict.

Fitzgerald brings us back to the clinic and shows that place of healing and professionalism in a petty light of jealousy and intrigue. Frau Kaethe Gregorovious seeks to discredit Dick Diver and succeeds in convincing Franz of his deficiencies. Dick is sent on a case to Lausanne where, to his shock, he finds Devereux Warren dying. Kaethe inadvertently tells Nicole, who rushes to join Dick only to find her father gone. Franz succeeds in pushing Dick out of the clinic after the embarrassing episode where a patient and his father accuse Dick Diver of being an alcoholic. But Dick is relieved; he has long been aware of the 'ethics of his profession dissolving into a lifeless mass' (Book Three, ch. III).

In each episode the original picture of Dick Diver and his perfect world disintegrates still further. This was not Dick Diver as Rosemary had originally encountered him, with a voice that 'wooed the world' and a 'hardness in him, of self-control and of self-discipline, her own virtues' (Book One, ch. IV). Fitzgerald, with an astute sense of symmetry, rightly takes the novel back to where it began, the Villa Diana and the Riviera. The connections with the past are made on the way home. They visit Mary North, newly remarried and now the Contessa di Minghetti. In the ensuing, somewhat bitter episode, Dick insults Mary. He remembers, at a subsequent meeting on the beach, how much time he had once given to 'working over her'. At home at the Villa Diana, Nicole recognises part of the truth and says that she has ruined Dick (Book Three, ch. V). There is another illuminating scene aboard the motor yacht, the reappearance of Tommy Barban and Nicole's growing disdain for the drunken, uncontrolled behaviour of Dick. This final book very much concerns Nicole and her emergent independence, as Fitzgerald concentrates more on her and Dick becomes increasingly isolated. He is in fact unnecessary, for, as he remarks to Tommy, she has become like 'Georgia pine, which is the hardest wood known' (Book Three, ch. VI). The narration further confirms this:

> Nicole had been designed for change, for flight, with money as fins and wings. . . . Nicole could feel the fresh breeze already . . . (Book Three, ch. VII)

For Dick, the return to the old beach is the most traumatic and effective moment. He almost fears the beach, 'like a deposed ruler secretly visiting an old court'. Dick scans this old domain looking for Rosemary, as Nicole grows more disgusted. They meet Rosemary, and Nicole assesses her just as she had been assessed by Rosemary five years ago. Dick looks for his lost youth in attempting unsuccessful stunts on the aquaplane. On meeting Mary North, once part of Dick's adoring circle, he finds that her reaction is coldly negative. Dick cannot recapture the glory of the beach, and Nicole leaves him still eagerly trying to pick up the remnants of his relationship with Rosemary. From both the narration and Nicole's own words and actions, it is apparent that Nicole is becoming more and more capable. She realises that she is nearly whole and almost 'standing alone, without him' (Book Three, ch. VII).

Enter Tommy Barban, the hero. Fitzgerald balances the physical strength and force of Barban against the intellect and will of Dick Diver. Tommy serves as the final escape that Nicole—and Dick—need. Fitzgerald focuses on the beauty of the setting of their moonlight bathe, and then on the reaction, the revolution within Nicole. It is a break that is made definite after one more chilling confrontation with Dick. Nicole wins her battle and, as the narration assures us, Dick has also won his: 'The case was finished. Doctor Diver was at liberty.' (Book Three, ch. IX). We are further assured, by the episode involving the escapades of Mary North and Lady Caroline as French sailors, that he has not changed: Dick still wants to be brave and kind, and most of all, to be loved: 'So it had been. So it would ever be . . . ' (Book Three, ch. X).

Indeed, so it had been. The words recall the beginning of Book Two and the young Dick Diver of 1919. Nothing has changed, Fitzgerald seems to be saying, and yet everything has changed. There are two more scenes before the psychological study closes. The first is in the centre of Cannes where Dick officially hands Nicole over to Tommy Barban. They settle this with little protest from Dick. The American selling newspapers to get his share of the wealth pouring into Europe floats ominously through the discussion. The narrative supplies the background with the famous annual long-distance bicycle race, the Tour de France, speeding by at the same moment.

The second scene is at the beach. Baby Warren is enormously satisfied by Dick's impending departure: 'When people are taken out of
their depths they lose their heads, no matter how charming a bluff they
put up.' (Book Three, ch. XII). Mary North tells Dick that he is still
liked and Dick tries to charm Mary, but inside himself he feels 'the old
interior laughter'. He cannot take it seriously. As the last symbolic act,
Dick blesses the beach.

At the end Fitzgerald describes Dick Diver just fading further and
further away into the recesses of New York State. He also moves away
from the possibility of any success of his own. His only gain is his
liberty.

Thus Book Three tells of the rise of Nicole's supremacy and her
values, as contemplated by Tommy Barban, and the completed demise
of Dr Richard Diver. Fitzgerald's scenes are less dramatic than those
that created the build-up in the first two books. This is a winding-
down, the greatest climax of the book having already occurred at the
end of Book Two with Diver's appalling experience in jail in Rome.
There is a sense of exhaustion about Book Three, which may come
from the destroyed character of Dick Diver. Time is important here
only in the lost youth of Dick, and the contrast between five years ago
and the present. What remains essential are the impressions of the
events upon the characters, the narrator and the reader. This is the verdict and the total evidence. Time has been broken up throughout the
book, disseminated in the events that seem to matter and recalled as a
life past in order of significance, not in order of years. The characters,
especially Rosemary, Dick and Nicole, testify to their own stories. The
narrative threads these together and supplies us with what they cannot
tell us. We finish with impressions of beauty and wealth, deterioration
and failure. We have the one certain piece of knowledge which Fitzgerald has wanted to convey—that Dick Diver's American Dream is
over and possibly never really existed. The early images of the Riviera
are just fleeting impressions against a developing background of dis-
integration and defeat.

Imagery

Imagery in *Tender is the Night* does much to emphasise Dick's nostalgia for the past, to highlight the anarchy and violence that came in the
aftermath of the war, and to point out the ills of money. Dick's initial
supremacy over these things and his control of his brave new world are
represented by the beach scenes of Book One. As Nicole says, it is their
beach made by Dick 'out of a pebble pile' (Book One, ch. IV) It is never
Nicole's beach and she hated it, 'resented the places where she had
played planet to Dick's sun' (Book Three, ch. VII). Remembrance of

62 · Commentary

the beach of the past brings home to Dick his total demise. He fears the beach: 'like a deposed ruler secretly visiting an old court . . . he could search it for a day and find no stone of the Chinese Wall he had once erected around it, no footprint of an old friend' (Book Three, ch. VII). Of course, it is this former fortress of power, where Dick dominated and gave so much to his friends, which is the last place he visits before leaving for ever for the small towns of New York.

If the beach is an image of Dick's strength, the garden is an image of Nicole's. Dick remarks fondly on how much she cares for it; this is her domain and Dick does not control her here. Dick also meets Nicole in a garden at the clinic (Book Two, ch. IX), the night that he tries to end their initial relationship. He thinks of her when he is away in Innsbruck, walking in another garden (Book Two, ch. XVIII). Nicole finds herself happy in the garden as the two men, Dick and Tommy, fight over her in chapter VI of Book Three. Later, for Tommy, she makes herself 'into the trimmest of gardens'.

Nicole embodies the elements of nostalgia, violence, corruption, money, sickness and even religion. The nostalgia that Dick continually feels for another America, one that before the war was less superficial and materialistic, is reflected in the countless images. The music scattered throughout the novel is one form that this takes. Abe North is a composer; he speaks of being 'plagued by the nightingale' (Book One, ch. IX). Music of any kind seems to be a reminder of conscience if not in its gaiety an ironic reflection of troubles. Nicole plays records for Dick when she is a patient at Dohmler's clinic, and even Dick's longing for Rosemary comes in with a musical cue: 'Tea for Two'.

This nostalgia also appears in the images of youth, such as those Abe North recalled or in the actual youth of Rosemary. There is Nicole's youth and beauty, the impression of which 'grew on Dick until it welled up inside him in a compact paroxysm of emotion' (Book Two, ch. V). Dick is constantly attracted to youth throughout the novel, and the aquaplane episode is a final pitiful attempt to regain his own youth.

Finally, nostalgia is shown directly by descriptions of the past. Dick notes the dignity of the enduring gold-star mothers, and pretends that everything is once again held together 'by the grey-haired men of the golden nineties who shouted old glees at the piano' (Book Two, ch. XIII). At home for his father's funeral, Dick kneels amongst his ancestors in the graveyard: 'These dead, he knew them all, . . . souls made of new earth in the forest-heavy darkness of the seventeenth century' (Book Two, ch. XIX). Finally, there are old comrades of the war and the illusions of America, the 'lies of generations of frontier mothers who had to croon falsely that there were no wolves outside the cabin door' (Book Two, ch. I). Above all, Dick Diver wishes this last was not lies, but truth.

The violence that marks the sharp break-up of that old world and the falseness of the American Dream are also portrayed through images throughout the book. Dick reviewed 'with awe ... the carnivals of affection he had given, as a general might gaze upon a massacre he had ordered to satisfy an impersonal blood-lust' (Book One, ch. VI). There is Tommy Barban, the epitome of violence and usurper of Dick's place with Nicole, always going to war. Chapter XIII of Book One has Dick and his party visiting old battlefields in France, land that 'cost twenty lives a foot'. There are the shots fired by Maria Wallis, 'echoes of violence', and Dick's arming himself for struggles to come, with the stick he carries 'at a sword-like angle'. The duel between McKisco and Tommy Barban is another act of violence, as is the murder of the Negro, Jules Peterson. Perhaps the most climactic violence is created by Dick himself in the quarrel with the taxi drivers, when his impatience erupts into 'violence, the honourable, the traditional resource of his land', and in the Rome police station when he knocks down the plain-clothes lieutenant (Book Two, ch. XXII). There are sexual images of violence as well. Tommy Barban tells Nicole of his experiences in America with girls who would 'tear you apart with their lips ... their faces were scarlet with the blood' (Book Three, ch. VIII). Finally, Nicole fights Dick back, no more a 'huntress of corralled game'.

Images of money and its corruption, linked to illnesses and a malaise of society, are also evident. As well as the Warren family, the newspaper seller who appears twice in the book also represents this aspect of the novel. The Warren money literally corrupts Dick and makes him inert in his work as well as weak with his own lack of wealth; he has allowed 'his arsenal to be locked up in the Warren safety-deposit vaults' (Book Two, ch. XVIII). There are other images of money; for example, it gives Nicole a long-awaited chance of independence: 'Nicole had been designed for change, for flight, with money as fins and wings' (Book Three, ch. VII). Nicole's 'white crook's eyes' seem to emphasise the corruption of money: 'a crook by heritage'. Finally, there is the absurdity of how a name that suggests wealth can bring great power and control: Dick tells the police that Mary is the grand-daughter of 'John D. Rockefeller Mellon'.

Images of illness and sickness also come to the fore in connection with the corruption of the American Dream. The clinics, and Nicole's own illness, caused by an incestuous relationship with her father, are obvious examples. Dick decides to be 'less intact, even faintly destroyed' (Book Two, ch. I). This comes to fruition when he acknowledges to Rosemary that he is 'the Black Death'. Again, another example of the superficial society of the twenties, Lady Caroline Sibly-Biers, is described as being fragile and tubercular. Amongst the company on the yacht in Chapter V of Book Three, Nicole notices the 'fierce neurotics'.

There are also images of Christianity, the antithesis of the materialistic society. Dick's father is a simple, honourable clergyman. Dick
remembers and imagines he himself 'was Crucified, Died, and was
Buried' (Book Two, ch. XVI). At Innsbruck he sees the statue of the
Emperor Maximilian which kneels in prayer. Even the corrupt Devereux
Warren takes to religion when he is dying. At Mary Minghetti's, Dick
hears two men chanting in an Eastern language and lets them pray for
him too. Nicole 'anointed herself ... crossed herself reverently with
Chanel Sixteen' (Book Three, ch. VIII). There is Dick's last, crucial
gesture when he blesses the beach.

Fitzgerald uses certain physical characteristics to illustrate character.
Nicole is very much her 'thick, dark, gold hair', hair that had once
been 'brighter than she', or similar to 'a cloud and more beautiful than
she'. The impression of a sheen, a halo, about Nicole is enhanced when
we hear of 'her face lighting up like an angel's'. Yet this same face is
hard, with green eyes, 'a viking Madonna'. Nicole is hard, bright and
metallic like her background of wealth and power.

Dick Diver's blue eyes are continuously referred to: 'the bright blue
worlds of his eyes', or they are 'cold blue eyes'. Later, these same eyes
are assaulted when Dick claims the police have put out his eye. No
longer is Dick's world that of bright blue; his eyes 'like search-lights,
played on a dark sky' (Book Three, ch. VI).

Fitzgerald uses moonlight as something romantic and positive, filled
with hope, sexuality and beauty. Rosemary 'lay awake, suspended in
the moonshine'; 'Her face had changed ... the eternal moonlight in it'.
Nicole looks precisely as if she is emerging from a wood into moonlight
(Book Two, ch. V); and later with Tommy, she swims 'in a roofless
cavern of white moonlight'. Indeed, Nicole has emerged from a dark
cavern, for her illness is always depicted as darkness: 'after my second
child ... was born everything got dark again', and 'thoughts about
Nicole, that she should die, sink into mental darkness ... made him
physically sick' (Book Two, ch. XXI). Finally, after what we later
realise was an attack of her illness at the party at the Villa Diana, the
guests help Dick to carry lamps out to the terrace: 'who would not be
pleased at carrying lamps helpfully through the darkness?' (Book One,
ch. VIII).

Style

Fitzgerald's style, considered rather self-indulgent in his earlier novels,
This Side of Paradise and *The Beautiful and Damned*, becomes more
controlled in later works such as *The Great Gatsby* and *Tender is the
Night*. There are still some self-indulgent rhetoric and flights of vivid
imagination in the latter, but Fitzgerald has progressed from his earlier

work, and considering the scope of *Tender is the Night* this was not an easy task.

What makes the difference is the greater amount of objectivity gained from the narrative as well as the use of an objective viewpoint such as the one utilised in Book One in the character of Rosemary Hoyt. This objectivity has an impact on style; the language is more precise and Fitzgerald does not indulge in excessively sentimental expression. It is less personal, and in a novel like *Tender is the Night* in which the subject-matter itself is so intensely personal, this is even more necessary.

Consider, for example, the passage in Book One, chapter VII ('Rosemary, as dewy with belief . . .') describing the atmosphere of the dinner at the Villa Diana. Fitzgerald gives a detailed impression of the charm of the Divers, beginning with Rosemary's point of view, and injects just enough satire to make the style more piquant. Notice the implied satire of 'Mrs Burnett's vicious tracts', the detail of the world filtering in from outside in the fireflies and the dog, the simile of the table as a dancing platform, and the careful diction with which the Divers are described as controlling their audience. There is even some irony as the passage continues in the use of simile with 'the faces turned up toward them were like the faces of poor children at a Christmas tree'. The passage is rich in Fitzgerald's attention to detail of atmosphere and nuance of feelings which is far greater than any detail of objects: 'the moment when the guests had been daringly lifted above conviviality into the rarer atmosphere of sentiment was over before it could be irreverently breathed'. Again, there is the edge of satire, which, like the objectivity of the narrative, helps to achieve a more accurate, less sentimental style, which in turn strengthens the force of the plot and the novel.

Fitzgerald does, however, introduce an element of nostalgia and sentiment into the novel in the thoughts and attitudes of the protagonist, Dick Diver. The difference is that the whole novel is not infused by the language that such an element might inspire. There is nothing very sentimental about Nicole's breakdown in the bathroom at the end of Book Two, for example, or Abe North's dissipated state at the railway station: 'dominating with his presence his own weakness and self-indulgence, his narrowness and bitterness' (Book One, ch. XIX). These words are not flattering or sympathetic. This lack of sympathy and an unwillingness on the part of Fitzgerald to give in to sentiment are what make Dick Diver pitiful, rather than tragic, in his decline. Even the theme of nostalgia exemplified by Dick is kept in tight control by the slightly satirical tone and objective style:

. . . on toward the Isles of Greece, the cloudy waters of unfamiliar ports, the lost girl on shore, the moon of popular songs. A part of

Dick's mind was made up of the tawdry souvenirs of his boyhood.
Yet in somewhat that littered Five-and-Ten, he had managed to keep
alive the low painful fire of intelligence. (Book Two, ch. XVI)

Here are the romantic descriptions that we often associate with Fitzgerald. Yet the word 'tawdry' stands out and the whole tone has
changed. This is the objective verdict, the dual understanding that both
pictures Dick's nostalgia and mocks it. It becomes a flaw in his character, something with which he has to contend and try to balance with his
intellect. The style emphasises the conflict between a 'littered Five-and-
Ten' and a 'low painful fire of intelligence'.

The loose construction of *Tender is the Night* allows for another
kind of style to enter into the novel. The impressionistic sense of time
and events allows for softer expressions of language. The opening view
of the Riviera (Book One, ch. I) shows a cool, refined descriptive
method. In metaphor and simile it is both vivid and discreet in a
'proud, rose-coloured hotel' with 'Deferential palms' and 'old villas
rotted like water-lilies'. There is 'the distant image of Cannes, the pink
and cream of old fortifications, the purple Alps'. This is a canvas rich
in both subtle shadings and strong colours. The passage has been carefully constructed to leave us with a sweeping impression that is both
elusive and concrete, and such snatches of soft, vivid impressions are
scattered throughout the novel.

These impressions expressed in evocative language add a richness to
the style which creates a fine, relieving contrast to the novel's harsh
realities of corruption and decay. It replaces sentimentality with some
reassuring beauty and does not override the objectivity that the style
also expresses. Fitzgerald's detailed descriptive passages of both beauty
and reality give greater depth to the themes and the story itself.

The style of writing—the manner and use of language—is very much
dependent on themes, structure, technique, imagery, plot, narrative
and characters in a novel. A finely tuned style makes the rest of the
ingredients work successfully.

Characters

Dick Diver

Dick Diver is the epitome of the well brought-up, middle-class, bright
young American. He is his father's hope back in Buffalo, New York.
Educated at Yale University and Johns Hopkins University, as well as
being a Rhodes Scholar at Oxford, he is a perfect example of American
brilliance and potentiality. Thus, as we see Dick Diver at the beginning
of Book Two, there is much to hope for from this young man.

His personality is full of contradictions—the wit and charm that Rosemary admires coexist with the analytical, serious mind of the psychologist. Forced by Nicole's illness constantly to put her personality back together, Dick also controls her. He spends a great amount of time influencing and 'working over' others. Yet he too falls apart, ruined by drink, the daily struggle of living with Nicole, and his own inability to live with the power and pressure of the Warren fortune. As he remarks, 'I've wasted nine years teaching the rich the ABC's of human decency' (Book Two, ch. XVIII).

Dick looks for ways out of his own psychological problems, through his work which is never completed, through a romance with Rosemary, through the clinic with Franz, and finally through freeing himself from Nicole. However, as a compulsive giver, he has given too much to Nicole and others. It becomes too late to save himself, and he fades into obscurity. The forces that Dick once controlled now control him. The only thing that he has succeeded in doing is making Nicole as strong as her background of money and power would suggest she ought to be. The young man of promise, so perfect in his moral upbringing and education, becomes an unsuccessful, alcoholic doctor with no real family or home.

Nicole Diver

As the daughter of Devereux Warren, Nicole is heir to a vast fortune. Her wealth and beauty are balanced against Dick's morality and intelligence. Nicole, made emotionally ill by an incestuous relationship with her father, leans heavily on Dick Diver's strength. She seduces Dick away from the security of his professional expertise by her sexual attractiveness; he is deeply moved by her beauty and youth. Later, she ensnares him with the total power of her wealth but is lonely 'owning Dick, who did not want to be owned' (Book Two, ch. XIV). Dr Diver, both professionally and emotionally, was what Nicole needed until her illness was completely beaten. As her sister Baby remarks, 'That's what he was educated for' (Book Three, ch. XII). Thus Nicole epitomises the greed of her capitalist background and the emptiness of money and beauty. Like her illness, these things also have corruptive powers. When she has taken all she can from Dick, Nicole is ready to match her own kind of force and power to the brute force and anarchy of Tommy Barban.

Nicole is part of Dick's dream in her beauty and money. She is the power of an emerging America. She is the proof that success can be attained. In many ways, Nicole Warren parallels the character of Daisy Fay in Fitzgerald's *The Great Gatsby*. She is also the hero's perfect ideal of woman, but, with the forces of youth, beauty and wealth behind her, she becomes a woman capable of great destruction. The idealism of middle America in its naïveté cannot see the corruption that can also exist in these forces, and is crushed by its own dream. Indeed, 'Nicole was the product of much ingenuity and toil.'

Rosemary Hoyt

At eighteen Rosemary seems to be another Nicole. A young actress from a middle-class background, she has been engineered into Hollywood by her mother. Like Nicole, Rosemary borrows her strength and character from other people, such as her mother and Dick, and from her various acting roles. She too lacks a core or a heart, yet her success has brought her all the glowing benefits of the American Dream.

To Dick, Rosemary is young and innocent, yet her sexual attractiveness is ever present. He appreciates being worshipped by Rosemary, mistaking, in his egotism, her youthful adulation for sincere emotion.

Rosemary, however, also proves vapid and less than innocent, as Collis Clay is quick to inform Dick. He finds himself obsessed with this knowledge, wanting Rosemary more; but already the dream has begun to fall apart. Rosemary at length says: 'Oh, we're such *actors*—you and I.' (Book One, ch. XXIV). Dick's romanticism about Rosemary has become as false as the promise of her beauty. She is glamorous Hollywood, but as much a façade as the film sets in which she works. In Rome, four years later, Dick tries to realise his dream of Rosemary but it has already gone. Like Nicole, she wants to take. She insists that she loves him, but 'what have you got for me?' (Book Two, ch. XXI). Rosemary is Dick's second chance at capturing his ideal but the episode with her merely helps to break him. He has become 'the Black Death.'

Tommy Barban

A mercenary soldier, half French, half American, Tommy Barban takes what he can from people by force. He represents brutality and the power that comes with it. He builds a fortune on money that he has initially made by fighting other people's wars.

Barban fights for and takes what he desires—money, a kind of power—and Nicole. His desire for her creates the duel between himself and the unfortunate Albert McKisco. The Divers make Tommy want to leave for war. Barban is ready to go to any lengths to defend Nicole's secret and her illness. Later, he is ready to protect and engulf her with this same animal vitality and force: 'she welcomed the anarchy of her lover' (Book Three, ch. VIII). Tommy Barban seizes his opportunity with Nicole as he has seized all else in life. He has waited until Dick has done everything he could do for Nicole. When he knows that Dick

Diver is finished, he assesses the matter with typical realism: 'You've got too much money. . . . Dick can't beat that.' (Book Three, ch. VIII).

Baby Warren

Baby Warren speaks from the comfortable pinnacle of an 'American ducal family'. Baby has little understanding of Nicole's illness, does not appear to know its basis, and merely wishes to keep Nicole safe like another family property or investment. She is against the marriage, but, when it seems inevitable, uses Dick as the doctor the Warrens had intended to buy for Nicole. She assumes Dick's motives are partially mercenary and makes certain he does not benefit financially.

Baby Warren lacks emotions: 'Her emotions had their truest existence in the telling of them' (Book Three, ch. XII). She does not react compassionately to Dick's disaster in Rome. Instead, she rescues him from jail with the fury of someone accustomed to power. She enjoys this opportunity of showing her control over Dick, pleased to gain 'moral superiority over him for as long as he proved of any use' (Book Two, ch. XXIII). When he does leave she is not sorry to see him go. She feels superior to him to the end: 'When people are taken out of their depths they lose their heads, no matter how charming a bluff they put up' (Book Three, ch. XII).

Abe North

Abe North, a light-hearted, unsuccessful, drunken composer, is a man who plays practical jokes. Rosemary first hears of him as the man who kidnapped a waiter in Cannes with the intention of sawing him in two (Book One, ch. I). He is also a typical failure. Rosemary learns that Abe had been a composer who had begun his career brilliantly but then had not written anything for seven years.

Abe, more than anyone else in the crowd, is Dick's friend. He handles the duel between McKisco and Barban, later telling Dick the story. They constantly joke together. But Abe is an alcoholic who cannot bring himself to go home to America. He manages to get mixed up with several Negroes over the incident of his stolen thousand-franc note, creating much trouble for all involved which ends with a murder. He seems to foreshadow what happens to Dick himself: ' "Abe used to be so nice . . . So many smart men go to pieces nowadays" ' (Book One, ch. XXII).

Dick Diver also has a brilliant start and also becomes an alcoholic, but he does not die the violent death which awaits Abe North in New York, where he is beaten to death in a speak-easy; instead he fades away pitifully. Both Abe North and Dick Diver are similarly defeated in the world of money and glamour in which they have tried to succeed.

Part 4

Hints for study

Points for close study

1. Consider the meaning of the American Dream and define what is Fitzgerald's ironic comment on it in the novel.
2. Show how Dick Diver's idealistic, romantic view of the world renders him incapable of dealing with it.
3. Trace the events that lead to Dick Diver's ultimate, climactic decline at the end of Book II.
4. Consider how the various narratives, those of the characters and the author, come together to create a more objective view of the total drama and aid us in reacting to the novel as a whole.
5. Nicole's illness initially makes her dependent on Dick, but not necessarily weak, for she is strong enough to take what moral and spiritual sustenance she needs. This leaves Nicole as the user of Dick's moral strength which in turn makes him weak. Show then how morality can create not merely strength but also weakness.
6. Fitzgerald has constructed *Tender is the Night* so that it is not all chronological but more a collection of psychological impressions. The order of events does not matter as much as the content and ultimate build-up of their impact. Show how this succeeds in making the novel more effective.

Specimen questions

Questions which invite discussion and argument

1. To what extent is Dick Diver a symbol of idealistic America and Nicole a symbol of the corruption of that ideal?
2. Is Rosemary Hoyt just a younger version of Nicole or is she somehow different? Does the Hollywood connection add something extra to her character?
3. Does Dick Diver approach the problems he faces in the plot of the novel from a position of moral strength or moral weakness?
4. Do the characters of Abe North and Baby Warren in any way parallel the characters of Dick and Nicole respectively? If so, give examples and suggest how these characters reinforce major themes in the novel.
5. How do the themes of love, power, corruption and money conspire

in *Tender is the Night* against the concept of the American Dream?
6. In what final incident is Dick Diver brought to a climactic defeat? As he is defeated, is Dick actually a hero or does he better suit the term 'anti-hero'?
7. What is the effect of Fitzgerald's constructing this novel so that it saves the explanatory background of the Divers until the second book? Does this serve to strengthen the book or does it confuse instead?
8. Discuss the use of irony in *Tender is the Night*.
9. Tommy Barban wins Nicole in the end. Is Tommy Barban a hero? If so, what kind of hero?
10. Consider the impact of nostalgia in the development of the conflicts in *Tender is the Night*.

Questions on content
1. Describe Rosemary's initial impression of the Divers on the Riviera in Book I. When does this begin to change and what events bring about this change?
2. Describe the main events of the Divers' romance as explained in Book II.
3. Trace the two different family histories of Dick Diver and Nicole Warren. Why does Baby Warren object to this marriage?
4. Suggest differences, if any, between Dick Diver as professional psychiatrist at the clinic and Dick Diver as host, entertainer, and husband of Nicole on the Riviera.
5. When do Nicole's feelings for Dick change? Recall the scene in which she makes the final break and show developments leading up to that point.

Context questions
Identify the speaker in each quotation and show its significance to the novel as a whole.
1. 'Oh, we're such *actors* – you and I.' (Book One, ch. XXIV)
2. 'You were scared, weren't you?' she accused him. 'You wanted to live!' (Book Two, ch. XV)
3. 'I want to explain to these people how I raped a five-year-old girl.' (Book Two, ch. XXIII)
4. 'You've got too much money,' he said impatiently, 'That's the crux of the matter. Dick can't beat that.' (Book Three, ch.VIII)
5. 'That's what he was educated for.' (Book Three, ch.XII)

Guidelines for answering questions

Here are some suggestions on how to set about preparing answers to questions, based on two examples.

To what extent is Dick Diver a symbol of idealistic America and Nicole a symbol of the corruption of that ideal?

This question has two parts and thus your answer should be constructed accordingly. First consider what a definition of idealistic America could be, and then look for examples of Dick showing these characteristics in the novel. Next comes the task of disproving Dick's beliefs in the character of Nicole. Look for examples of Nicole's corruption, and juxtapose these to the examples of the ideals in which Dick initially believes.

By first defining any main terms in a question, and then developing an answer, as defined by the question, with appropriate examples, you will find that you can organise your answer efficiently and logically. So you should always pull apart and identify the main concerns of a question before trying to answer it. Make sure that your conclusions are backed up with examples from the text.

Another point in approaching a question is to consider what connections the subject of the question has with other aspects of the novel. For instance, should you use the characters to answer the question, or information about style, theme, structure or technique? You will find that there will always be a connection of some kind. The question about Dick as a symbol of idealistic America and Nicole as a symbol of its corruption is easily connected not only to the characters of Dick and Nicole, but to such themes as Fitzgerald's view of money and power. Similarly, a question on theme attaches itself to characters. See how easily you could start with part of the answer to the first question in answering this next one.

How do the themes of love, power, corruption and money conspire in *Tender is the Night* against the concept of the American Dream?

Dick Diver embodies the potentiality for, and certainly believes in, an idealistic America, one in which the American Dream in its purest form is possible. To Dick, Nicole is love, power and its implied corruption, and money. He loves for love, but is nevertheless ensnared by money and its influence. This destroys his idealism, his own version of the American Dream. On the surface Nicole represents it, but in her control of him and in the actual reality of what she is, she shows this dream of his to be merely illusion. Thus the themes of love, power, corruption and money can best be shown to destroy the American Dream through the characters Fitzgerald has created to illustrate these forces.

Again, terms must first be defined. Examples can be followed through as they are taken from characters, and, further, as a part of style or technique. You could show how Fitzgerald expressed the themes in imagery. It is helpful to remember that a novel breaks down into component parts, and attacking any one of these can aid you in answering a particular question. What is essential is to determine which aspects of the novel will help most in answering a specific question. To do this, you must go back to the beginning: (a) define the terms; (b) identify the concerns of a question; (c) logically assessing the component parts of the novel, determine which aspects help to explain these concerns best; and (d) back up your argument with specific examples from the text.

Specimen answers

To what extent is Dick Diver a symbol of idealistic America and Nicole a symbol of the corruption of that ideal?

Dick Divers believes in America and the American Dream. He is a product of the nostalgia for the bygone era of his father, with honour, courage and integrity as its great virtues, yet he readily faces his 'whole new world'. As is stated in the beginning of Book Two, he possesses the 'illusion of eternal strength and health ... the essential goodness of people ... illusions of a nation'.

Thus Dick sets out to make his mark, to be a great psychologist. In Nicole Warren he sees what he thinks is the ideal of the American Dream – and a means by which he can realise his own dream. On the surface she is young, beautiful and rich, the daughter of an American capitalist, Devereux Warren. A member of a prominent Chicago family who have successfully fought for their position and won, Nicole has, however, been corrupted by an incestuous relationship with her father and has fallen mentally ill as a result. Her family also does not believe in the values in which Dick's poor preacher father believed. They believe in using others for their own ends, in using the skills of a doctor like Dick to keep Nicole safe – 'That's what he was educated for.' – and in buying what they need with their money. Nicole is the ultimate product, the grand-daughter of a horse-trader with 'white crook's eyes'. She uses up Dick as she and her family have always used any other resource available to them. She is the very image of the American Dream and yet Dick finally realises, when he has given what he can, that this was just another illusion. His idealism is ground out of him until he fades into the quiet, obscure world of small towns in upstate New York. Nicole's corruption has resumed its face of strength

instead of illness: 'now made of – of Georgia pine, which is the hardest
wood known'. Dick's idealism has undergone an enormous attack and
he is now the 'Black Death'. An idealistic America, an American
Dream, has crumbled under the weight of its corrupt reality as exemplified in Nicole Warren Diver Barban.

Do the characters of Abe North and Baby Warren in any way parallel
the characters of Dick and Nicole respectively? If so, give examples
and suggest how these characters reinforce major themes in the novel.

Abe North seems to suggest Dick Diver's own decline before it ever
happens. He is the talented composer, precocious in an auspicious
beginning, who has written nothing for seven years. Instead he has
become a light-hearted ornament of society – a comic and a practical
joker. He is an alcoholic and Dick's great friend. As his gaiety and
alcoholism increase, his natural gifts apparently wane and are burned
up. Abe cannot seem to find the thread, to get back on the boat to
America and on with his career. Sadly, he is heard of in New York,
beaten to death in a speak-easy. This is a terrible reality to Dick, who
mourns for his lost youth that Abe North in part represented. In fact,
Dick Diver does in several ways resemble the unfortunate North. As
Doctor Diver, he began his career with one book published and plans
for another. Yet this material is never completed; it stays on his desk
throughout his decline. We are reminded of it, even at the last, when
Dick has left Nicole and the Riviera behind. On his desk are a pile of
papers, 'known to be an important treatise on some medical subject'.
Dick also becomes an alcoholic, and his alcoholism speeds the decline
further, through such episodes as his fight and beating in Rome. Both
are men of great potential who choose to live in a superficial, idle
society that ultimately consumes both them and their talent.

Baby Warren is more completely a Warren from the beginning than
her sister Nicole. She does not have Nicole's illness, which makes
Nicole seemingly vulnerable. Yet she is like Nicole and what Nicole
becomes again after the final renewal of all her strength. She is a Warren and believes in her right to power and money. She believes that
people should be used as both she and her sister use Dick. Baby Warren
feels that people have their place and that she is above most of them.
She thinks it fair that the Warrens should buy a doctor for Nicole, just
as she thinks it only right that the Warrens should have the power of an
'American ducal family'. Dick's virtues and talents do not matter. It is
money that matters; in it lies the power to own Dick, to buy a clinic and
to give herself and Nicole endless luxury.

Baby does not need any real emotions, just the knowledge that she is
right and finally has 'moral superiority' over Dick and his ideals. She is

completely ready to support Nicole in her move for independence from Dick who is discarded for the more brutal force of Tommy Barban.

Baby and Nicole are indeed one of a kind: Nicole's illness, in other terms a symptom of her corruption, has perhaps initially made her seem weak and more introspective; but, in the end, she is no different from her sister. Indeed she may be worse, as she has a greater, more subtle capacity for using people under the pretext of rightful need.

Thus both Abe North and Baby Warren respectively complement the two main characters and help to underline the consequences of the themes of money, corruption and power. Abe North, like Dick Diver, is crushed by these things, while Baby Warren, like her sister Nicole, is nourished by them.

What is the effect of Fitzgerald's constructing this novel so that it keeps the explanatory background of the Divers until the second book? Does this serve to strengthen the book or does it confuse instead?

The technique of postponing the truth about the Divers, of not immediately revealing Nicole's illness and the resulting embattled position of Dick, allows Fitzgerald first to construct an example of a perfect world of the 1920s. Superficially, all would seem to be well. The 'whole new world' of Dick Diver and his society of friends would appear to work. The American Dream of wealth, beauty and youth seems to be intact.

Fitzgerald has the freedom to present a glamorous scene on the French Riviera. He is able to view this apparently perfect world through the young innocent, Rosemary. She is a part of the American Dream, the middle-class girl who makes good in Hollywood. She is, therefore, both naive and sympathetic to the superficial values which the Divers represent. She does not want to find faults but rather to believe that the man in the jockey cap and his 'viking madonna' wife are the finest people. Dick Diver seems magical to Rosemary because of his ability to transform a quiet beach into a glamorous place of frolic. This is a man who can handle all kinds of individuals, who can richly entertain at the Villa Diana such various types as Al McKisco and Tommy Barban. His beautiful wife completes the picture and complements his own wit and charm. Here is beauty, money and the magnetic energy of youth all utilised to a positive end.

Initially, the picture is romantic and flattering. By withholding the facts until the second book, Fitzgerald can gradually hint at the truth and carefully pull apart the pleasant composition. The duel between Tommy Barban and Al McKisco is the first concrete breakdown of this harmony. Of course, the first hint of this breakdown and the cause of the duel is the mysterious, awful thing seen by Violet McKisco in the bathroom of the Villa Diana.

Everyone apparently recovers from this dramatic climax. Rosemary is swept up in the mad gaiety of Dick Diver's parties and outings in Paris. However, the mood does become more serious. Rosemary and Dick embark on a romantic involvement. Dick, originally the man who could handle everything, finds the attempt at an affair with Rosemary too much to handle. He hints darkly at his complicated love for Nicole as a result of her problems.

The total answer is not yet to be supplied. Instead, we see the Divers' perfect world slipping further into confusion. Abe North, their great friend, is shown to be a dissipated failure. He strikes out bitterly at Nicole at the railway station in Paris. He is unable to face his life. He leaves Paris only to return immediately, and then manages to entangle himself in a dispute with some Negroes in Montmartre. Out of this confusion comes further disaster: the Negro businessman, Jules Peterson, is murdered in Rosemary's room at the hotel. The Divers become involved in removing the body and Nicole cracks under the strain. Rosemary witnesses her fit of madness in the bathroom of the Divers' suite.

By withholding the background material, Fitzgerald is able to create the great climax in Nicole's breakdown. He is also able carefully to let the cracks form in the façade of the American Dream as exemplified in the Divers as Rosemary had first observed them. Finally it crumbles, as Dick's control and power subsequently crumble in Books Two and Three of the novel. Now Fitzgerald is ready to take the reader back to Zurich and back to the beginning of the relationship between Nicole and Dick Diver. The reader has viewed the Divers at their best and also at their worst. We are ready for the facts and the explanation as to what has gone wrong. It is really the beginning of another story, for it shows just what kind of battle has always been faced by Dick Diver. It prepares us for his final defeat. Fitzgerald's novel has not been weakened by the information withheld but rather strengthened in its impact. As we would learn about any society or individual, we learn the surface first, a deeper knowledge comes later. Fitzgerald's story of the failure of the American Dream and the specific failure of Dick Diver is reinforced by the contrast between the original, harmonious impression and the subsequent harsh realities.

Part 5

Suggestions for further reading

The text

SCOTT FITZGERALD, F.: *Tender is the Night*, vol. II, 'The Bodley Head Scott Fitzgerald', The Bodley Head, London 1961. This is the original version, first published by Scribners in 1934. There are no notes, but in volume I of the series there is a general introduction by J.B. Priestley.

SCOTT FITZGERALD, F.: *Tender is the Night*, Scribners, New York, 1961. Reprints the original version of 1934.

SCOTT FITZGERALD, F.: *Three Novels*, Scribners, New York, 1953. The second book is *Tender is the Night* and this is the version revised by Fitzgerald in 1939.

SCOTT FITZGERALD, F.: *Tender is the Night*, preface by Malcolm Cowley, Penguin Books, Harmondsworth, 1970. This is the revised version of 1939.

Other works by Fitzgerald

This Side of Paradise, Scribner's, New York, 1920.

Flappers and Philosophers, Scribners, New York, 1921.

The Beautiful and Damned, Scribners, New York, 1922.

Tales of the Jazz Age, Scribners, New York, 1922.

The Great Gatsby, Scribners, New York, 1925.

All the Sad Young Men, Scribners, New York, 1926.

Taps at Reveille, Scribners, New York, 1935.

The Last Tycoon, edited by Edmund Wilson, Scribners, New York, 1941.

The Crack-Up, edited by Edmund Wilson, New Directions, New York, 1945.

The Stories of F. Scott Fitzgerald, introduced by Malcolm Cowley, Scribners, New York, 1951.

Afternoon of an Author: A Selection of Uncollected Stories and Essays, introduction and notes by Arthur Mizener, Princeton University Press, Princeton, New Jersey, 1957.

The Pat Hobby Stories, edited by Arnold Gingrich, Scribners, New York, 1962.
The Letters of F. Scott Fitzgerald, edited and introduced by Andrew Turnbull, Scribners, New York, 1963.

Biographical and critical studies

CALLAHAN, JOHN F.: *The Illusions of a Nation: Myth and History in the Novels of F. Scott Fitzgerald*, University of Illinois Press, Urbana, 1972.
KAZIN, ALFRED (ED.): *F. Scott Fitzgerald: The Man and His Work*, The World Publishing Company, New York, 1951.
MILLER, JAMES E.: *The Fictional Technique of Scott Fitzgerald*, Martinus Nijhoff, The Hague, 1957.
MIZENER, ARTHUR: *The Far Side of Paradise*, Houghton Mifflin, Boston, 1951.
MIZENER, ARTHUR (ED.): *Scott Fitzgerald: A Collection of Critical Essays*, Prentice-Hall, Englewood Cliffs, New Jersey, 1963.
Modern Fiction Studies, I, No.1 (Spring 1961). See its checklist of Fitzgerald criticism.
PIPER, HENRY DAN: *Scott Fitzgerald: A Candid Portrait*, Holt, Rinehart, & Winston, New York, 1963.
TURNBULL, ANDREW: *F. Scott Fitzgerald*, Scribner's, New York, 1962.

The author of these notes

GRETCHEN L. SCHWENKER was born in Princeton, New Jersey and received her university education at the College of Wooster, Ohio and at the University of Stirling, Scotland, where she completed a thesis on the *Autobiographies* of W.B. Yeats.